The Fashion Show

RENZO BARBIERI

The Fashion Show

Translated from the Italian by Joachin Neugroschel

LYLE STUART INC. SECAUCUS, N J

First published in Italy under the title La sfilata

Copyright © 1985 by Gruppo Editoriale Fabbri,
Bompiani, Sonzogno, Etas S.p.A.

Translation copyright © 1986 by Lyle Stuart Inc.

Published by Lyle Stuart Inc.
120 Enterprise Ave., Secaucus, N.J. 07094
In Canada: Musson Book Company
A division of General Publishing Co. Limited.
Don Mills, Ontario

Queries regarding rights and permissions should be
addressed to: Lyle Stuart, 120 Enterprise Avenue,
Secaucus, N.J. 07094

Manufactured in the United States of America

Library of Congress Cataloging-in-Publication Data

Barbieri, Renzo.
  The fashion show.

  Translation of: La sfilata.
  I. Title.
PQ4862.A67263S413   1986   853'.914   86-14487
ISBN 0-8184-0409-4

*To Claude and Catherine Taittinger
and especially to their champagne*

Chapter 1

"Oh, my God!"

Who was going to break the news to Ciaccio? Rick was gone, as in "very gone." His bed hadn't been slept in. The closet door gaped open, all the hangers bare. The drawers were totally empty, not even a hastily overlooked sock remained. Rick was gone, as was the complete set of Gucci luggage, and everything else for that matter.

Patrizio looked at himself in the mirror. He had a habit of tossing his mane-like blond hair whenever he was pleased with himself and he tossed his hair now. He picked up a tray that had been left on top of the TV and headed with it to the kitchen.

He certainly wasn't going to say anything to Ciaccio (a.k.a. the Big Turk). Let Alvise do that, he thought as he headed across the vast living room toward the kitchen.

He turned off the oven so the roast wouldn't dry out. Then

he dialed the number of Ciaccio's company.

"Irone Fashions."

"This is Patrizio. May I please speak to Signor Alvise?"

A moment later, Alvise—Ciaccio's aide, assistant and chief bottle washer—was on the phone, a voice that seemed to have a slight edge of hysteria built into it. "What's up, damn it! You know—"

"I know you're very busy, Signor Alvise. To get to the point— Rick has cleared out!"

"Cleared out? You're crazy!"

"He's gone, I tell you. Lock, stock and Gucci."

"How can that be?"

"He must have left in the middle of the night. I got up at seven this morning. I would have heard him leaving . . ."

"Are you *absolutely* sure?" Alvise's voice took on an added layer of anxiety.

"Do you think I'm making this up? Come and see for yourself."

"I can't believe this. O.K. I'll be right over."

Alvise slammed down the phone. This was the last straw. The collections were just two months away and of course Ciaccio was under incredible pressure, working his butt off, creating models, selecting fabrics, colors, furs, leathers, everything.

Outdoors, a watery sun was trying to break through the pollution haze of Milan. "*Mamma mia*, it's a furnace out there!" Alvise scurried along in the shade of the old palazzo walls. Wired with irritation, lost in a dozen different thoughts, he headed toward Ciaccio's home on Via Montenapoleone.

Alvise had never cared for Rick, California surfer incarnate— all white teeth, blond hair with muscles for brains. He had in fact taken an instant dislike to him, that day when Ciaccio discovered Rick modeling. Ciaccio, on the other hand, was as instantly hooked. He had invited Rick to dinner the same evening. Humpy, yes, in his overobvious fashion. But so tacky, so vulgar, so provincial. He even gave off the quaint air of liking women. Clearly a

12

primitive. But those were Alvise's thoughts. In the ten years he had been working for Ciaccio he'd never seen him tumble so fast and so completely. A week later Rick Stanton was installed in the penthouse on Via Montenapoleone, cock of the walk, so to speak.

And now catastrophe—worse, apocalypse. As recently as yesterday, Ciaccio had confided to Alvise that life without Rick wasn't worth living.

Alvise took the elevator up. Patrizio, in white trousers and a canary-yellow jacket, greeted him at the door, dripping with feigned concern.

"Well?" asked Alvise.

"Check for yourself. The nest is empty." Patrizio ushered him into the agreeable coolness of the six-thousand-square-foot apartment. Floor tiles, carpeting, all of impeccable taste, all obviously from the House of Irone.

"Don't just stand there like a fool. Go and see if you can find any trace of that ungrateful creep!"

Wearing a short-sleeved, white silk robe, the Big Turk had been shut up in his studio since five A.M. All four young assistants also wore the same monk-like garb. Practical, yet chic at the same time.

The black marble table was shaped like a big I—for Irone. The top was covered with virtually everything from drawing paper, sketch paper and the like to scissors, paste pots, Magic Markers and, most important of all, sample swatches of every conceivable color and texture.

This room was the heart of Irone creation. The walls were covered in a kind of black felt. There was one very solid sheet-metal door. There were no windows. The Big Turk (Ciaccio to his fans, Saladin the Fierce to his enemies) used an ivory intercom to make contact with the outside world—not even a telephone to strike a discordant note.

If anything, the one discordant note in this bastion of high elegance was the rocking chair.

"It used to belong to John F. Kennedy," the Big Turk would

explain. "After his death, Jackie wanted me to have it."

So far, no one had ever called his bluff on that one.

Ciaccio loved to rock for hours, his lanky body swaying back and forth. It carried him back to his childhood—the seesaw in his grandfather's orange grove, the merry-go-round in the town square on Sunday afternoons. To indulge his nostalgia with a rocking chair was not enough—he had bought an old carousel, vintage 1910, fancifully adorned with all kinds of gilded figures. It still worked perfectly. This he installed in one of the large halls of his baronial villa in Brianza.

The rumor was that he came up with his best ideas while riding the carousel. Atop a black bay, or sprawled out in a gondola, he would sketch out evening clothes, leather jackets, chic sweaters.

People may have jeered at this fancifulness on his part, but the millions of dollars and billions of lira that poured into his till every year had a way of bringing the jeering down to whisper level.

With one hand he pushed his curly hair out of his eyes, drew a huge X negating a drawing handed him by one of his assistants and then pressed the button on the intercom.

"Has Rick called?"

"No, *Cavaliere*." He'd longed for that title half of his life—only last year had it finally been obtained. No matter how down he was, being addressed by it always gave him pleasure.

He looked at his Gerald Genta: it was noon. Rick usually called by ten-thirty.

"Send for some more coffee. I'm going upstairs for a moment," he said, getting up.

A few moments later, in his private sanctum, he was nervously dialing the number at the apartment.

"Is Rick there?"

"He's gone out, *Cavaliere*," Patrizio replied, cleaving technically to the truth.

"I suppose he's on his way here," Ciaccio concluded and hung up.

14

"I don't think so."

Alvise had materialized in front of the desk. Alvise, the mainspring of Irone Fashions.

"What are you talking about?" Scowling, Ciaccio shot him a baleful look.

"It would be better, I think, not to hide it from you. Rick split, probably last night sometime. Destination: Unknown."

Ciaccio gaped at him, bewildered, his arms propped on his desk, his lips quivering.

"That can't be. Is this some kind of a joke?"

"Before breaking the news to you, I went to the apartment and investigated it myself. I can assure you, this is no joke."

Ciaccio turned white. One hand moved to his heart. His eyes turned up in his head and he collapsed.

"There goes the collection," Alvise sighed. "I knew that excuse for American manhood would jinx us." He bent over Ciaccio, who lay motionless, his head to the side.

"Oh, my God! Water! Help! Water! Help somebody!" Alvise had finally lost his cool. "We're ruined . . . *ruined!*"

Alvise Mittaglia was a born Richelieu. He liked running things without the pomp of having to sit on the throne or attend ceremonial functions. He was Ciaccio Irone's right hand—more precisely, his entire right arm. It was he who had built the company and kept pushing it on to further exploits. People outside Bel Reame—Milan's fashion district—could think Ciaccio Irone ran the whole shebang. Alvise was concerned with the substance— he was the real heart and soul of the enterprise. Ciaccio was the titular head, he the motive force.

"Goddam! Goddam! Goddam!" Alvise's voice reverberated through the huge billiard room.

Once again Alvise was called upon to save Ciaccio. A mess, just like all the others. Ciaccio was an absolute pushover for a combination of an athletic body and a big piece of meat.

Alvise picked up a cue stick. "Where am I going to find Rick

Stanton?"

He talked to himself, striking the white ball, missing the red by a mile. This was his way of letting off steam—solitaire billiards and lengthy soliloquies.

He liked talking to himself. Sometimes he did it when other people were around. No one knew for sure how much was affectation, how much unself-conscious nattering.

"Maybe he's run off to Tokyo with some small Japanese businessman who's aroused a taste for the exotic in him. Maybe he's developed a yen for the yen. How am I supposed to find one stupid Californian in a world where jets fly everywhere?"

The white ball finally hit the red. He put the red ball back in the center of the table and gazed at it, deep in concentration.

"I don't like having to depend on luck. I've got to reason this out carefully. Who would be able to unearth a twenty-year-old kid, with unusual good looks who could be anywhere on the planet?" He rubbed some chalk on the tip of his cue. "Rick's American. It would seem logical that the investigation begin at his hometown and fan out from there. I'll need at least the FBI or at least the CIA. Or a detective agency."

He thought of Tom Ponzi.

"Think big, Alvise, think big."

Replacing the cue in the rack, he picked up the phone and called his office. His secretary, Vale, answered. She was the most efficient secretary in all of Milan—certainly the only one who could speak French, German, English and Arabic.

"Vale, get me the New York Pinkerton Agency." Alvise suddenly remembered Rick Stanton was a native of Palo Alto, California. "No, wait, get me their San Francisco office."

This particular mess was going to cost a fortune. Ciaccio wouldn't mind. It would be a deductible fortune.

Why had Rick Stanton taken off? He couldn't possibly have fallen in love with a woman or another man, could he? The possibility of a fat cat, Oriental or Occidental, really didn't hold much water either. No one was more generous than Ciaccio in rut.

16

Why, on Rick's twentieth birthday, Ciaccio had given him a burglar-proof chain for the bike Rick was unaccountably fond of. A solid gold chain, eleven pounds, designed and cast personally by Pomellato.

Alvise sighed. And to think that any Big Jim (Italian slang for an American male model) could be had for two dinners at Bice and an occasional silk shirt. Yet here was American Rick, having hit pay dirt, on French leave. Someone must have talked him into it. Someone intent on screwing up Ciaccio but good. And that someone could only be one person: Lorenzo Diovisi.

The jangling telephone interrupted his stream of invective at that hemorrhoid of a competitor.

It was Vale. "The Pinkerton Agency has no office in San Francisco."

"Try L.A."

"I just did. They're on the line."

Vale was the best secretary in Bel Reame, no doubt about it. Alvise smiled. He had stolen her from Lorenzo Diovisi.

It was nighttime in L.A. but one of the directors was still in the office. He was delighted to speak with the head administrator of Irone Fashions. His name was John Covelli, obviously Italo-American. Obviously also, Alvise was convinced, Italian style. Alvise listened patiently to his compliments, which lasted quite a while. Finally he managed to assign him the job of tracking down Richard Stanton, age twenty, last know residence: 69 Via Montenapoleone, Milan, Italy.

"We'll find him," Covelli guaranteed, "even if we have to turn America upside down!"

Chapter 2

*D*iana Rau, wearing a bathing suit, was sitting between Francesca and De Ferraris. They were in chaises longues by the villa's swimming pool. It was Sunday afternoon. Friends, journalists and fashion models of all four sexes were circulating in the huge gardens.

Francesca was wearing a minuscule flesh-colored bikini. She was detailing her husband Kiki's amorous adventures. He was on the verge of a total nervous collapse because, after two solid months of importuning and trickery, he still hadn't seduced the Sardinian servant. On Diana's right, dressed in a linen and cotton suit, De Ferraris was talking about the fashion business, which wasn't doing as well as last year.

"PR costs keep going up. Made in Italy fashions need continuous PR, nonstop promotion."

"Kiki spies on the poor Sardinian day and night. His name

is Efisio Porcu. Kiki calls him his little piggy."

"We've got France by the short hairs. America adores us. But the market still isn't as good as it was five years ago."

"He's short, thick-set, he's got a very large head and absolutely no forehead whatever. Kiki claims he has the virility of a Neanderthal."

"We have to keep up the competition on all fronts."

"I've never seen Kiki so far gone. He's in a constant state of blue balls."

"If the market's depressed, we should get the government involved. We should ask for special considerations, subsidies."

Diana was bored. She removed the sunglasses behind which she had taken refuge, and stood up.

"Your husband's up, the market's down. There's no justice anywhere." She dove into the pool. Pier Damiano was just returning from the golf course with a few friends.

Diana smiled at him as she lifted herself out of the water and onto the edge of the pool. She admired her lover's elegance and beauty. But she felt no desire for him. Perhaps after a few months with anyone the fire dies down. Perhaps also because Pier Damiano was too beautiful, too composed even, or especially, in bed. That's it, perhaps he was too perfect; leaving the bathroom, radiant, never a wart, never a shaving nick, hair perfectly in place. Is it possible he combed his pubic hair? His fucking technique was equally blameless and without blemish. When he came he permitted himself a discreet restrained moan. Diana imagined his sperms goosestepping in rows toward her uterus.

And yet, many people envied her for having this man.

Diana's gaze wandered over to the large park that cut into the forest, one of the last green spots in Brianza that had not been overrun by factories or swallowed up by real estate speculators.

"A marvelous park," observed Alvise Mittaglia. "So is what's left of the forest. It sounds like it's filled with nightingales."

Evening was setting in.

"Come on, I want to show you something." Diana got up and

preceded Alvise along a narrow path.

"The hunters have slaughtered so many birds and animals in Brianza that even the protected areas, like this forest, are depopulated. Here are my nightingales."

Alvise stared at the object hanging from a wire, half-hidden by the leaves of a linden tree.

"A transistor loudspeaker. What you're hearing are recordings of caged nightingales, which, we all know, sing far more beautifully than their free siblings, because they feel so sad."

"You have a poetic soul."

"I'm no poet," Diana retorted. "I'm the exclusive Italian representative of these loudspeakers. They're made in Germany."

"Well then, you have a remarkable business instinct," Alvise laughed. "How many have you sold so far?"

"I've supplied half the gardeners of Italy. But my best customers are penthouse dwellers, like your friend Lorenzo."

Alvise sneered. He still rankled every time someone referred to Lorenzo Diovisi as his "friend". He himself had convinced Ciaccio to call him that during interviews. Otherwise, the journalists would discover the silent feud between the two giants of the so-called Italian style. One said, "I admire his courage." The other said, "I appreciate his integrity." "There's room for both of us," they chorused. In reality, they loathed each other.

"I came here tonight just to talk to you about my friend, Lorenzo," Alvise said to Diana's back as she led him back to the pool.

She pretended to be hurt. "And not for my party?"

Alvise said nothing. He and Diana went way back. He knew that the grand villa rented from Count Carandetti, the party, the whole evening including the nightingales were professional tools for this highly skilled PR woman, she who had once been the reigning queen of the fashion models. Although she freelanced now and then, she was under contract to Irone Fashions.

"What's happened?" Diana asked. She knew Alvise well enough to know something was wrong.

"Rick has walked out."

At first, Diana couldn't remember who the hell Rick was, so, stalling for time, she pointed at the bougainvillea covering the southern wall of the villa and said, "That's the only bougainvillea that's adjusted to Brianza's climate." Meanwhile her mind was racing. Ah yes, Rick, good-looking American, blond crew cut, blue eyes, the one Ciaccio was crazy nuts about.

"Maybe he ran off with Lorenzo," Diana joked.

"If only! Then I'd at least know where he is. No, the problem is, we've got to get him back immediately, if not sooner. Ciaccio's gone into a tailspin. I had to send him to a sanatorium, for a sleep cure. He's positively suicidal. It's going to take a miracle to get the collection ready in time."

"You want me to get Rick back for you?"

"The Pinkertons will take care of that. All you have to do is tell the press that Ciaccio Irone is exhausted and on doctor's orders is taking a rest cure. Most important, stress how lucky we are that Ciaccio designed the entire spring-summer collection and checked the models before he was checked in."

"How much of that is true?"

Alvise felt the tears come to his eyes. "Let me put it this way: If that beachboy doesn't turn up soon, we're all up shit creek. If Lorenzo gets wind of anything he'll be delirious with joy. I'm sure he's got wind of something—he's throwing one of his Dolce Vita parties at his villa. He says merely to escape the Milan heat. But I *know* it's to celebrate the fall of the house of Irone. I'm in a no-win situation. If I go, I'll be a laughing stock. If I don't go, they'll definitely know something's up and suspect the worst. If none of us goes, the newspapers will be onto us. So the only solution is that you go and defend Ciaccio and the collection. I can count on you not to lose your cool."

"O.K. Alvise. I'll save your ass and make sure no one laughs at Ciaccio."

Diana opened the window. The sound of chirping crickets—

22

real ones—filled the room. She closed the window and stood there, her nose against the cool pane. She stared out at the moonlit park. She loved the moon, and she liked doing girlish things, like pressing her nose against the glass. She had a girlish face with a snub nose. All life is a game, she thought.

"The crickets have finally returned to the park!"

She turned her head to look at Pier, lying there, reeking absence. Naked, lying supine on the bed, there were plugs in his ears, his sleep mask in place. His way of relaxing completely—not sleeping, just relaxing.

She walked across the room and sat in the armchair next to the bed, unwittingly crumpling all his neatly laid-out clothes. She stuck out her tongue and thumbed her nose at him. She made a face, gnashing her teeth. She flicked her tongue obscenely. How boring.

She suspected that, cold as he was, Pier didn't totally withdraw from the world. The night mask had to have a hole in it somewhere through which he saw everything, including her recent gestures. But he remained quiet, impassive. Life could be easy if, like Pier, you didn't have feelings.

She looked at the glowing watch on the dresser—two A.M.

She wasn't sleepy. She lay down next to Pier. He was awake, she sensed—he never slept when he was "relaxing." He was awake, but far away, farther out than usual. He didn't seem to be breathing. His arms lay at his sides, his fingers open, his legs slightly apart, his lips closed. His penis lay at an angle, canted off to the left—a discordant note.

Diana often wondered what she saw in Pier Damiano—besides what everyone else saw, that is. Their sex life was as mechanical as it was active and conventional. He would undress and instantly be poised and ready. The same act, the same way—never any variations of position, never being swept away with uncontrollable emotions. Once, she asked him to enter her from behind. He did so with the same good will, technique and aloofness he used regularly—he'd make the perfect flight atten-

23

dant. One good thing: He was able to hold back reaching climax until his coincided with hers.

He ate the same way. Diana had never seen him pee, but she was sure she knew how he approached that task as well.

Diana felt like an instrument with only one function in Pier's life. She started reaching out for his penis but lost interest halfway.

She closed her eyes. She had to get some sleep. Relax, rest, push away disturbing thoughts. Disturbing thoughts have a way of furrowing a woman's brow, especially a woman who only the week before had celebrated her thirty-ninth birthday. Not celebrated, exactly; observed would be more accurate.

Her lids were half closed. She made herself close them all the way. She was starting to drift off. She always had pleasant dreams.

Chapter 3

They had taken over Bel Reame—a rectangle between Via Manzoni, Via Senato, Corso Venezia, Piazza San Babila, and Corso Matteotti. Via Montenapoleone cut straight through the entire district. Here were the most beautiful stores in Milan, the most elegant and exclusive shops, as well as the workshops themselves where the new ideas behind every new law of fashion were being produced. The huge mansions of Ciaccio Irone and Lorenzo Diovisi were both located near the very heart of Bel Reame—one on Via Sant'Andrea, the other on Via del Gesù. Both houses were formerly owned by scions of book publishers who had totally dissipated their patrimonies and were compelled to sell.

"Today *we're* the culture producers," Ciaccio had declared to an interviewer.

The interior designs of the two palazzos revealed the diverse personalities of these kings of fashion. Diovisi had knocked out virtually every interior wall, so living area flowed into work area—in fact, everything flowed into some other area. White walls, low and pale beige chairs, the floors blond woods of various kinds. Lorenzo worked in an area containing a huge gray plastic-laminate table, mirrored wardrobes, mirrored walls. There was always a vase of fresh flowers about. The only decoration was a Baroque fresco by Tiepolo, looming on the ceiling over Diovisi's desk.

The bedroom area was even more austere with its enormous platform bed, covered with many brightly colored silk pillows. Here too there was only one painting—a naked Saint Sebastian by Teo Angeli. The martyr bristled with arrows down to the groin; his very young face, not unexpectedly, had a look of intense suffering.

"It's an orgasm," Teo had confessed to Lorenzo. "When I painted it I insisted the model masturbate. That was the look on his face when he came."

Ciaccio Irone's house was completely different. No light colors, no vast open spaces, no simple lines. In the entrance hall one was greeted by Roman busts—dozens of marble originals, all confirmed by noted experts in the field. The inlaid ceramic flooring created perspective illusions usually confined to high Renaissance paintings. The ceilings, the bathrooms—everything was some form of valuable antique. Ciaccio's bed, for instance, was a fifteenth-century fourposter of carved wood, its canopy covered with frescoes.

"And a black silk dressing gown always lying in careful disarray on the quilted bedcovers to feign a disorder probably suggested by the interior designer as a nice accent," Diana Rau thought when she first saw it. She was now moving through the city in her Volvo station wagon thinking about the contrasting styles of Diovisi's and Ciaccio's homes. They were probably the only Italians left these days who could afford such profligate luxury. Their businesses had annual turnovers in the hundreds of millions of dollars. Besides, heads of business in other industries wouldn't have had the nerve to flaunt such wealth quite so shamelessly.

26

Diana was headed toward Lorenzo's country house, a patrician villa on Lago Maggiore. He had bought the twenty-room mansion from an old noble family that had come down in the world. He reduced the number of rooms to fifteen, increased the number of bathrooms from two to twelve, thereby transforming it into *the* summer playground of the Milanese crowd.

Diana slowed to light a cigarette. She was in no hurry. The party would go on until dawn. All she had to do, really, was to show up, represent Ciaccio and assure people who were crass enough to ask that God was in his heaven and all was right with the world. An easy job. She didn't give a damn about Ciaccio, Diovisi or any of the others. She was only biding her time till the exquisite right moment when she herself would spread her wings. She had more than enough experience, good taste, imagination, and money to build a fashion empire, just as Krizia and Mila Schon had done.

"Just a few months and the name Diana Rau will be as famous as Ciaccio Irone and Lorenzo Diovisi. I have everything I need to get what I want." She giggled. "I'm even talking to myself like Alvise."

The villa was illuminated by lights strategically placed all over the park. Clusters of torches and Chinese lanterns created an interplay of light and shadow everywhere. A skyrocket now and then took off from the roof of the mansion, sliced across the sky and slowly descended toward the water. The lake beautifully reflected all the lights.

Diana parked her Volvo under the two grand staircases that met at the entrance to the villa. Here she began to hear party sounds—voices, alughter, music. That was how Lorenzo's parties began, orderly and elegant. They usually wound up in total bedlam.

She got out and passed along a walk lined with an enormous bush of white hydrangeas. The blossoms looked phosphorescent because of the halogen lamps strategically placed every ten feet along the flowerbeds. A hand reached out from the bush and grabbed Diana's shoulder. Caught by surprise, she let out a gasp of fear. A man emerged. Letting go of her arm, he clasped her around the waist.

"Haven't you ever been voilated among the hydrangeas, angel?"

Diana recognized Filippo Ranetti, nicknamed the Empress, for his regal ways, his softly regal ways. He was dressed all in white—to match the hydrangeas, perhaps?

"Never, she answered with a smile.

Ranetti, loosening his grip, took on a look of immense sadness. "Alas, neither have I."

"Walk me inside. We cut quite a figure together."

She rather liked Ranetti, the king of furs. He provided fabulous creations for royalty (what was left of it), movie stars (what was left of the real thing) and everyday millionairesses (very much in the ascendant).

Not handsome, not ugly, not tall, not short, not skinny, not fat, Ranetti was distinguished by what he wasn't. A kind of negative presence. The one thing he was was autocratic. He once slapped a countess who arriv ed at a pary in a rival's fur.

"I can't," Ranetti said, pointing at the hydrangea bush. "I have to stay in my hiding place."

"What are you doing in there anyhow? Spooking arriving guests?"

"No. I'm here for Giovanni, one of the servants, to come and piss here. Lorenzo told me this is where he pees."

In parting, Diana leaned over and kissed the Empress on the cheek. He smelled of makeup. "At least for now," Diana thought. She must remember not to kiss him goodbye later.

It was a splendid night. The stars over the lake suggested infinity.

She entered the vast, white salon. Mirrors everywhere reflected and re-reflected the guests in passing.

Only a few people greeted her with smiles. Surprisingly,

kissed, hugs, darling-how-*are*-yous had been abolished the year before by Diovisi. His edit was: "Those things are nothing but expressions of decadence or, to put it another way, much too Hollywood."

It was time to decide which group or which lone wolf to join up with.

Everyone was here, except, of course, representatives of the Irone faction, which Diovisi, head of the Milanese clan, labeled provincials.

Lorenzo Diovisi (Lorenzo the Magnificent) was leaning against a window post, sipping champagne and listening to Ubaldo Baraldi, known as the Little Lord.

Impeccable was Baraldi's middle name. It was rumored that his undershorts were so cleverly slit in the back that he didn't remove them even when he had to poop. If this was a fashion statement, the world had yet to decipher its precise meaning. He was probably as megalomaniacal as one can be in the fashion world, which is saying quite a lot.

His shows always took place in original settings: famous squares, grand museums, stately theaters. "The only thing he's left out is the Municipal Cemetery," Giorgio Armani once quipped.

Everyone in Bel Reame had a nickname. Some flaunted it—for instance, the Little Lord. Others didn't know about theirs, or at least pretended not to know—for instance, the Empress. Still others would have been mortally offended—for instance, Aldo Stembiati: small and delicate in all his features, he was the Stud Mouse.

Some gave themselves a nickname, or *nom de guerre*—for instance, Maria Teresa di Montenapoleone. Her real name was Teresa Vaca (cow), but God help you if you called her that, at least within her hearing.

The Cow was gossiping with another member of the Milanese clan, the Handsome Priest (secular name, Tatino Faveri), the celebrated designer.

Diana recognized the usual baker's dozen of female editors

29

of the fashion press. To a woman, they were remarkably ugly and terribly dressed. The flock of foreign female models, the so-called Barbies, and the herd of their male colleagues, the Big Jims, were biding their time, waiting to pick someone up to get through the rest of the evening with privately.

None of the models, male or female, was well-known.

They had all just arrived in Italy, their knapsacks stuffed with their photographs. They were ready and willing to do anything to make it.

There was Aldo Coppola, the hairdresser; Nando Chiesa, the makeup artist. There was the publisher of *Chic*; there was the plastic surgeon who specialized in altering buttocks (the joke around town was, his autobiography would be called *From Cellulite to Cellulose*). There was Florabella Maghi, gossip columnist, surrounded by her sycophants (since she was one-legged, people would say, "Ah, there's La Maghi, with all the world at her foot"); there was the choreographer Silo Piglio (bilingually nicknamed Tutu); a beautician named Cello (his ability to fit between any pair of thighs was legendary); ex-fashion models; PR specialists; upcoming (or down-going, depending on who you asked) fashion designers Adriano Tenori, Luluccia Fondelli, Mosquito and Chiavotti; Marta Fagotta (nicknamed Deep Moat); a tennis pro or two, a soccer star or two, a politician (Socialist, of course) or two; Mister Elegance Checco Bolognese (nicknamed Beau Baloney); a few playpersons from the Caffe Roma; also a group of Italian fashion starlets. Of these, two stood out more than the others—one, Inna Delfino, a niece of Diana's, was a stunning brunette, the other a stunning redhead.

"Hi, Auntie, what are you doing here, slumming?"

"You tell me."

"I was invited by Ruggero Valenti. Wasn't that sweet of him? He promises he'll call me for Lorenzo's next show."

Inna had dropped out of school and plunged into a career of modeling, Diana's former success inspiring her. All Diana's efforts to dissuade her had been futile. "I want to be famous like

30

you," Inna declared. She did indeed seem to have everything going for her: a beautiful, original face, high, defined cheekbones, a perfect forehead, the appearance of intelligence; also, she was unusually tall for an Italian.

Diana capitulated. She would help her niece all she could, sparing her whenever possible the exorbitant dues. Diana had seen a lot of wholesome girls fall completely by the wayside. Maybe they had one good season. Then, if lucky, they vanished into some kind of marriage; if unlucky, into some kind of slough, either one of drink or drugs or calories. Not even the movie world devoured so much humanity so swiftly or ferociously. A lucky actress could drag on for decades; a lucky model maybe had five good years. The first crease, the first hint of fat, the first clouding of the eyes (whiskey or cocaine or sex abuse all showed first in the eyes) and the butterfly was pinned to the page and the page was turned. Other faces, other svelte figures took their place. At the moment the most desirable were the Americans, with their pale faces and long legs, and the blacks with elongated bodies and sex-starved faces.

"Fuxia is going to work for Diovisi too," Inna said.

Fuxia Taylor, the redhead, looked around. She was beyond it all, totally spaced out.

In doubt as to whether Fuxia understood enough Italian or whether she was in a world where lucidity and comprehension had no meaning, Diana whispered to Inna, "Don't let people see you hanging around her, she's always whacked out or drunk or stoned and sooner or later she's going to get burned."

"I like her. Besides, if everything works out, I'm invited to spend Christmas at her home in Manhattan."

"She's also a lesbian."

"Surely you're not going to moralize like a stuffy old aunt, are you?"

Even though Inna had said it with a giggle, Diana felt her heart skip a beat. "Stuffy" and "aunt" she could live with; it was the "old" that cut to the quick.

31

Leaving the salon she walked along a corridor papered with magazine covers featuring Lorenzo Diovisi and his creations.

She opened a door and found herself in a bedroom. The room was dark, barely lit by a small lamp off in a corner. All Diana could make out was that the bed was covered in black sheets and the wall behind the bed was a huge mirror. All she could tell was that there were only two people, but which combination of two was beyond her grasp. They didn't stop. She said nothing. She tiptoed past them toward what looked like the door to an adjoining bathroom. It was. She stepped in and closed the door. The room was filled with ferns and mirrors. Lorenzo had a positive fetish for mirrors, for the simple reason that it made admiring himself such a handy and easy task, no matter where he was.

Diana gazed at her image in the mirror, focusing on her body. She stood there, surrounded by the white of the porcelain fixtures and the green of the recently misted ferns. She saw a very tall blonde with a slender face and full lips. Slowly, she began to strip. An uncomplicated operation. She was wearing a simple red-silk tunic-like gown—a Ciaccio Irone creation, of course. All she had on underneath was a kind of abbreviated loincloth—a tiny triangle covering her pubic area held in place by a thin string that ran up her buttocks. Thus, the silk of the dress didn't reveal any unsightly intimate apparel as she moved about.

Naked she was even more beautiful. Though with the passing of the years her breasts had begun to sag slightly, her legs were still slender, her hips graceful and her skin taut. There was the barest hint of cellulite on her buttocks, but any woman over the age of sixteen had that problem.

Reassured, she got dressed again and left the bathroom, tiptoeing past the very self-absorbed duo on the bed.

In the hallway she ran into Lorenzo Diovisi himself, in a lively and expansive mood, a cigarillo in the corner of his mouth.

"Come on, Diana, let's go out on the terrace." He led her, putting his arm about her waist.

Outside, the night was warm and soft. There was the scent

of flowers on the air, which was humid from the lake. From inside, the din of voices and music could be heard dimly.

"Isn't the view magnificent?"

An L-shaped fleet of boats lit by Chinese lanterns was drifting across the water. L for Lorenzo.

"Too bad Ciaccio's in a clinic," he murmured, leaning against the marble balustrade. Diana was instantly on the alert.

"The poor thing's exhausted," she replied.

"We all work ourselves to the bone. And that's what comes of it."

"Preparing the collection took it all out of him."

"I gather he was only about half finished." He stared at her intently.

"I don't know where you got that idea. Gossip, pure and simple. The collection's done. He was way ahead of schedule." Diana spoke calmly. Alvise would approve of her approach.

Diovisi mustn't even suspect that Ciaccio was a nervous shambles, let alone how much of the collection actually was unfinished.

Diana thought she glimpsed a hint of disappointment in Diovisi's face, but she wasn't sure. How much of what went on at Irone Fashions *did* he know?

Lorenzo took her hand. "I'd love to have you do PR for me," he grinned. "Think about it. Enough of this shop talk. Let's go over to the pool. I want to show you what I've done with it."

"Don't tell me you've filled it with piranhas and plan to throw someone in."

The Olympic-size pool was surrounded by 1200 square yards of imported tiles. It lay right in the middle of the park in a clearing made by the cutting down of a grove of 200-year-old cypresses. It was reached by small, winding gravel paths lined with rosebushes.

Masses of paper lanterns, suspended on invisible wires, lit the area. Tonight the pool had been transformed into a skating rink, and a crowd of skaters was darting about in costumes closer to bizarre than chic.

There were several small tables and chairs on one side of the pool, attended by waiters in full livery. Diana and Lorenzo sat down at one of these.

Diana, although inured to outlandishness by years of experience in fashion, found herself gaping at the skaters whirling around. The music was provided by a small ensemble of violinists.

A big bodybuilder, all in pea green, his face heavily made up, a pink boa floating after him fluttering around his neck, did a slalom that had everyone applauding, everyone that is, who wasn't scrambling to get out of his way.

A red goblin (this was Diana's guess) with bells on his cap darted up from behind and gave the bodybuilder a knowing pat on the butt.

"Keep your hands off the merchandise!" the bodybuilder shouted, turning around to chase the impudent troll.

Roman warriors, Cleopatras, Borgias and Medicis glided across the ice. All of them were in a high state of at least giddiness, whether due to a party mood or drugs was impossible to tell.

"Make way for the Countess from Hong Kong," cried a Sophia Loren lookalike.

"Tell the truth, don't I look like Raquel Welch?"

"My guess would have been Bea Arthur."

"I'm a *diva*, a *diva divina*," called out either a transvestite or Maria Callas back from the grave.

"Call the Pretorian Guards. I'm in a mood to have an army march over me."

"Be nice to me and I'll let you shave my legs later."

"Poor Amanda, still looking for the right thumb to suck."

"Ooh, how handsome you are in this light. You're like Count Dracula, you must never go out before sunset."

"Well you never saw him naked. Either he's got the tiniest cock in captivity or the biggest clitoris."

"I thought they called her Cat because she gossiped so. It turns out that with the right combination of drugs in her, she can lick her own asshole."

"Someone get me a glazed chestnut. Either I've got the munchies or my diaphragm failed again."

Backward, forward, in tempos ranging from the mazurka to the waltz, jumping, gliding, they skated on, a crazy quilt of shouts and laughter, bitchery and scorn.

Several groups were approaching from the villa, all thick-tongued, all walking too carefully. The drinks and drugs were taking effect.

"I can remember the good old days in Monte Carlo."

"Can you? What do you remember best—the early Empire beds or the late Empire orgies?"

"I thought of bringing my wife but then I thought, what if I find some gorgeous hunk here tonight?"

"Where's Lorenzo? How did he pull off such a coup as this skating rink?"

"Piece of cake. Two generators working steadily for three days. Of course the workmen charged him double for overtime."

"There's a perfect instance of how we all live under the yoke of the proletariat."

Someone skated by naked with a cigar in his mouth and one sticking out of his ass. No one offered him a light.

The onlookers milled about, drinks in hand, flowing apart and back together in new configurations.

"What do you do in real life?"

"Let's put it this way—I'm into hustling."

"Oh really, buying or selling?"

"For the longest time I thought Herpes was a fashion line, like Hermes."

"I finally found something that turns my husband on—a chastity belt."

"For him or you?"

"My husband always knows the right accessory for everything. Whenever he screws me in the bathtub, he insists I wear my emerald earrings."

"I'm not ashamed to say I have only one goal in life; to spend as much money as I can."

"This isn't my scene."

"What kind of scene is your scene?"

"Take some Tiger Balm, add some sour cream and let your imagination run riot."

"I just realized what all this reminds me of. A ball at the court of Louis XVI, in Versailles, on July 13, 1789."

"Such a memory you have, *cara.*"

Eyes sparkling from too much alcohol, Tatino Faveri staggered over to Diana and Lorenzo.

"Maria Teresa di Montenapoleone is signing bedsheets," Faveri announced.

"Maybe it's territorial, like wolves peeing on a tree."

"Or a dog returning to its vomit."

Tatino pulled out a hundred-thousand lira note and rolled it into a straw.

"What's that, the tip?" Diana joked.

Ignoring her, Tatino produced an authentic sixteenth-century chiseled gold French box. It was filled with crack, the high potency cocaine. He poured a little on the back of his left hand, placed the makeshift straw in his left nostril and gracefully sniffed in the coke.

"He certainly has a flair, a style about his snorting," Diana whispered to Lorenzo.

"It can't be healthy," Lorenzo whispered back. "Think of all the germs there are on money."

Diana got up and in parting kissed the top of Lorenzo's head. "See you later. I want to go inside."

Having completed her assignment for Irone Fashions, she could now go to work for herself. She wanted to find Kao Misokubi. She had glimpsed him in a cluster of Barbies earlier. Misokubi was one of the richest men in the world. He owned a chain of department stores throughout the Far East.

For years now, Diana had been running into him at fashion

36

shows and parties and he had always courted her, but with a bit of excess refinement, as if he needed her permission. Diana preferred more decisive, aggressive men. If nothing else, it saved time. Flattery, telephone calls, flowers were for adolescents. She preferred men who gave the impression they were seconds away from ripping off her panties.

She had changed her mind about Kao because of her friend Alfio's computer. Alfio loved computers. As a lark, he'd programmed into his computer a list of all the men Diana could marry who would help her get her own fashion line off the ground. She could trust Alfio like a brother.

She needed at least two billion liras to start off on the right foot. That limited the field severely, right there. A man who could bankroll her and provide a steady cash flow. Ideally, a husband who would be so busy with his own enterprises he wouldn't be around much. It would be all right if he slept with other women, as long as it was done discreetly, and he wouldn't mind if she now and then played around as well, equally discreetly of course.

The computer was fed all the data on the ten men who were within Diana's reach. Every entry had a plethora of information culled from every imaginable source, including private detectives hired by Alfio's office, the largest computer distributor in Italy. The computer whittled the field down to one: Kao Misokubi.

Alfio said, "I hope you're not a racist."

"Quite the opposite. I like being taller than the man I'm with."

"Well then, go for it. He is, after all, a billionaire in several international currencies."

"He's been after me for two years. I hope he's still interested and hasn't gotten tired waiting."

"Ask him."

Diana was skeptical. "Where am I going to dig him up. Last I heard he was cornering the market in mainland China."

And now, as if by magic, tonight, Kao had turned up at Lorenzo's party. Clearly a sign from above.

I should have consulted Vanessa before coming here, Diana thought to herself as she entered the main salon and was joined by the Empress. He immediately started telling her the story of his encounter with Lorenzo's servant. Vanessa was Diana's fortune-teller. She advised Diana on all matters, great and small, suggesting when and how to act.

"I don't know how long I lay in wait in that damn hydrangea bush," the Empress said. "I was beginning to feel like a hydrangea myself. Well, to make a long story short, the kid turns up. There's no one around. He's quite a slim fellow. Anyhow he reaches into his fly and pulls out this thing. I've never seen anything so large on a human in my life and believe me, I've gotten around. Well worth waiting for. It was so big that . . . it was so big that . . ." The Empress couldn't come up with an apt phrase. He merely smiled ecstatically.

Diana meanwhile was looking all around for Kao. He seemed to have vanished. He loved parties. Maybe he was on an upper floor.

"And then what happened?" Diana asked.

"He pretended not to notice me. He pissed all over my shoe. Look, it's soaked, all the way through to the sock. I didn't want to spook him, in case he really hadn't seen me, so I grinned and took it like a man."

"Or a hydrant," Diana interjected.

"I'm going to hide there again in a little while. Next time he comes to relieve himself I'll show him what real relief is like." The Empress left Diana and went over to Fuxia Taylor, who was looking very much as if she needed to lean up against something.

Out on the terrace Diana found Inna, who was skillfully resisting Paolo Sgargaglia, a handsome playboy a bit over the hill. He wore his usual reinforced-heel shoes—he had an inferiority complex about his short stature. His hair was on the long side, curled by Bruno Vergottini. Before and above all else, Paolo loved his Rolls-Royce. Paolo claimed his mother gave birth to him in the back seat of a Rolls. Wicked tongues claimed that the only sex

38

Paolo found truly satisfying was when he jacked off behind the wheel of his Rolls. Referred to as "the great heartbreaker" in the gossip columns he was a womanizer more in the breach than in the deed. No woman could hope to replace the Rolls as the center of his life. Therefore, Diana didn't mind seeing him chat it up with Inna. If Paolo had his eye on her, it meant he thought she was an up-and-coming model, destined to reach the top.

"You're still the most beautiful woman in Milan, Diana," Paolo said, kissing her hand. Diana noticed only the "still." "You've got only one serious rival: your niece."

Diana thought the compliment was well chosen—perhaps Paolo wasn't as stupid as she thought he was. She left the two of them and moved on in her search for Kao—he was nowhere on the terrace.

Diana went through the salon and on into the garden. Kao was not there either. She was beginning to fear that he might have left the party. Nevertheless, she decided to go up and check out the second floor.

She finally found him in a room on the third floor. He was watching a late evening newscast. In the blue light cast by the black and white set she recognized the back of his head leaning against the couch he sat on. She could make out his smooth black hair, combed à la Valentino, the back of his delicate neck.

She entered and silently closed the door behind her, puzzled why he'd be watching a news program at a party. He seemed to be paying close attention to the blather of the two blow-dried anchorpeople.

Deciding to surprise him, she came up behind him and put her hands over his eyes. "Guess who?"

It was then that she noticed the woman kneeling between his thighs, her head in his groin, bare breasts floating out of her decolleté, the mass of blonde hair bobbing up and down rhythmically. Diana's "guess who" now seemed the act of someone near to crazy.

The Barbie, for it was an American woman not three weeks

in Italy, removed her mouth from Kao, looked up and said, "Are we playing Knock, knock?"

"I don't know what's going on," Kao answered.

Removing her hands from his eyes, Diana looked down at Kao and smiled a smile she hoped would be interpreted as sophisticated nonchalance and hurried out the door.

Kao said, "Positions everybody." And wondered whether the phantom had really been Diana Rau.

The salon was deserted. Everyone was out on the terrace, in the garden or down by the pool. In the garden people were applauding Fuxia Taylor who was weaving slowly back and forth in what appeared to be a trance, naked. In the sky, the rockets kept on exploding. Reaching the lip of the wharf, Fuxia attempted a pose on tiptoe, then vanished over the edge into the lake.

"Someone fish her out. Otherwise, in her state, she'll drown," Lorenzo called out.

"Don't ruin a good story!" Maghi called out, already motioning her photographer to the end of the wharf.

It seemed no one cared to brave the waters, not even the waiters who were imperturbably passing around the drinks trays to the guests.

"If she drowns, we'll cause a scandal, we'll all end up in jail," Aldone Stembiati called out. But he didn't head for the wharf either. They were beginning to give up hope for Fuxia when she suddenly surfaced next to the wharf and crawled to a rocky strip of beach. She was soaking wet, this being 1985, in a combination of water and oil stains. A waiter ran over with a bathrobe and was cheered as the hero of the hour.

While the others started strolling back to the villa, Kao appeared next to Diana and asked, "Was that you a little while ago?"

"No, it was my doppelganger, trying to rescue you from the sordid experience of just one more cheap thrill."

He laughed. Maybe it was lucky for her she had surprised him with that Barbie. Diana needed some excuse to change the tone of her relationship with Kao. She wasn't about to say, "I love you because you are the only man who's capable of financing my own fashion company." It was far better to let him think she suddenly got an attack of spontaneous jealousy on finding him embedded in someone else.

They left the crowd. In a quiet room on the second floor, he offered her some crack from a solid gold snuffbox. Diana was tired, her legs ached, her eyes felt hollow, her skin felt taut and tense. She breathed in the magical snow and leaned her head back on the couch. In a few seconds, her fatigue vanished. It was replaced with a desire to jump up and dance, swim, have sex.

Diana let Kao kiss her on the lips. With one hand, one very expert, searching hand, he explored her long legs all the way up to her groin. His hand caressed her blonde pubic hair.

"I'm the only truly natural blonde in all Milan," she muttered. It wasn't a joke, it was true. She had no need to dye her pubic hair. She was the most desirable blonde in Bel Reame. At least three men had squandered fortunes for that downy hair, another had killed himself, and many without number had adoringly knelt down before her, ready to give their lives for just one kiss. All that was left now of that celebrated past glory was her reputation and that still much-desired tuft of hair.

But for how much longer? She shivered uncontrollably. Just a month ago, while doing her toenails, she had casually glanced at her groin. To her total horror, she had glimpsed a hair that was much too pale. White! She had pulled it out violently, deliberately trying to hurt herself, to injure her body, which, though still beautiful, was daring to send out such mortal signals. It was only a single hair and so discreetly hidden in her lush blonde growth that it would very easily have eluded all notice but the most scrupulous—until, that is, some chance lover of hers would discover it. She could hear the news spreading throughout Bel Reame now—blown up, exaggerated, embellished: Diana Rau is turning gray between her legs.

She stopped Kao's hand as it reached for further intimacy.

He was breathing harder and harder, his eyes, like a cat's, were growing smaller and smaller, just two slits between the lids.

"No, not here. Not like this."

Her usual words when a rejection was only temporary, when it was a prelude to something more important. And Kao Misokubi, like all the other men, believed her. "Tomorrow night would be better. We'll dine at Toula."

"I'd prefer St. Andrew's. It's more intimate."

"It's a deal."

Diana hesitated. "Don't you play with me. The truth is, I'm afraid to go out with you. You could suddenly take off for the other side of the earth and I . . . " She broke off in mid-sentence. She hoped she wasn't overdoing it.

Everything was all right. Kao was smiling happily.

"I'll call you tomorrow."

Finally removing the hand he had nestled in between her thighs, he got to his feet.

Now Diana could return to Milan. If she stayed any longer she might get sucked into some kind of gang bang or other. Better to vanish like Cinderella. She had carried out her two assignments to perfection, one for Mittalglia/Irone and the other her assault on Kao Misokubi. Lingering now could lead to mistakes.

Diana walked down the stairs, passing two couples. A man and a women who were French kissing, two males who were absorbed in jerking each other off. She intended to leave by the back way, get her car and melt into the night.

Crossing the billiard room her eye fell on an odd sight. A Barbie was sitting on the green table, crying her eyes out. Her hair was a mess, her legs and breasts uncovered. Leaning against the wall was the playboy Alberto Tassi, whose father owned a huge racing-car organization. Alberto was busy masturbating to the sight of the crying Barbie. Diana ignored them and they her.

Inna must have left already, probably with Fuxia Taylor. Inna knew damn well what Fuxia was after. Despite occasional flings with men, her weakness was for beautiful women, a weakness that might work against her someday.

Diana decided to warn her niece again. If Inna had to go to bed with women, she should at least do it with the right ones and not waste her time with the Fuxia Taylors of the world—Barbies who were too much in love with the combination of whiskey, coke and parties.

Chapter 4

The Big Turk had left the Lugano clinic a week ago, after completing the sleep cure. On arrival at the clinic with Alvise playing nanny, a physician sent him into oblivion with a needle in the right buttock. His last words before closing his eyes were:

"Where's Rick? I want Rick!"

When he awoke 120 hours later, his first words were:

"Where's Rick? I want Rick!"

The sleep cure had failed to cure. Ciaccio hadn't forgotten his Big Tom. Maybe he had even dreamed about him and was now more in love than ever.

"Well? I want an answer."

"I've got the Pinkerton Agency looking for him. If they can't find him, then no one can."

"I bet you think he's nothing more than a cheap slut and not worthy of me."

Alvise said, "Well, to tell the truth, I don't think he's a *cheap* slut. He's not a dime a dozen. Maybe a million liras a dozen."

"I don't care what you think, Alvise, if I don't get him back I'll abandon the collection, I'll abandon everything."

They had returned to Milan in an ambulance, sirens shrieking. Back at home Ciaccio immediately fell into a deep melancholy.

There was a hunk, a dream hunk, waiting for Ciaccio in his bed. Alvise had paid a considerable sum of money to hire him. A mulatto, twenty years old, he was the son of an African man and a Norwegian woman. His skin was dark, his eyes were blue. He had been Sheik Yullah's favorite for two years.

But the gift was useless. As soon as Ciaccio laid eyes on him he went into a tantrum. The gorgeous gift lay there naked, already aroused. Ciaccio acted as if he had found a scorpion in his bed. Alvise had stationed himself outside the bedroom door, hoping to overhear the beginning of a new romance. Instead, he had to dash into the bedroom and rescue the mulatto from Ciaccio's iron grip—he was trying to strangle the poor boy.

"I want Rick!" Ciaccio shouted throughout the night.

While most of Bel Reame slept, the lights burned in Alvise's bedroom far into the night. Alvise had taken the mulatto into his own bed—no sense letting the mulatto's services go unused, they were too expensively bought. After the boy had fallen asleep, Alvise stayed up thinking of possible ways of curing Ciaccio. It was a measure of his failure to come up with practical ideas that he fell asleep thinking, I could try taking him to Lourdes.

The next morning there was a cable in the mail. It was from California.

RICK STANTON WORKING IN LA AS EXTRA IN TV FILM. LIVING WITH ANOTHER EXTRA. SEND INSTRUCTIONS. (SIGNED) BOB MANLEY, PINKERTON AGENCY.

Alvise offered up a silent prayer of thanks. He had to talk to Rick, talk him into coming back, and that wouldn't be easy. Either he had run off for his own private reasons or someone unknown had paid him a hefty sum to take off.

Locking himself in his office so as to be undisturbed, or overheard, he placed a call to Manley, who luckily was in the office. Manley gave him the details of his tracking down Rick. The kid had spent a couple of days in New York with a former lover of his, an off-Broadway actress. Then he had gone to see his family in Palo Alto. He seemed to have a lot of money. The extra job had fallen in his lap—it was arranged by his roommate. He hadn't been looking for work.

They were living and working together—the movie was a made-for-television film on child abuse. Manley, on his own initiative, had had a talk with Rick. His impression was that someone in Milan had been the motivating force in convincing him to leave Italy.

Alvise wondered, Could that motivating force be Lorenzo Diovisi? Was there any chance in getting Rick back to Milan?

"I think so," Manley replied. "All you have to do is make him a bigger, irresistible offer. I suspect, however, his demands are going to be sky high."

After hanging up, Alvise began to formulate a plan of action. Manley was not the right one for the job of trying to persuade Rick to return. He either had to do it himself or send a surrogate equally adept and quick-witted. He ruled himself out—someone had to mind the store. Diana Rau might do, but for the last several weeks she'd been acting funny, distracted. Could she be going into a premature menopause? Whatever it was, she would be less reliable than usual. Alvise needed someone who was not only a friend but loyal and incorruptible.

"Marco! Just the man for the job."

Marco had 32 wristwatches, thirteen of them gold Rolexes. Often when he would decide to spend the evening at home, he'd open the safe where they were kept, take them out and arrange them on the carpet. Then he'd sit back and beam with pleasure.

The most recent acquisition, a Jaeger-le-Coultre, was on his wrist. The strap was a light pale-yellow pigskin, a color which Marco adored. He may even have bought the watch primarily for its strap. He held his wrist under the lamp that stood on his desk, admiring the watch. It had character, a refined feeling, an elegance, and the strap suited it perfectly.

The phone rang.

"Hello." There was a touch of annoyance in his voice. He hated being interrupted when he was alone with his watches.

"Marco?"

"Enza? Where are you calling from?"

"Portofino. Why aren't you here? Did you forget?"

"I'm coming tomorrow."

"What's holding you up?"

"I came home late . . . . I haven't eaten yet . . . . I may even skip dinner. It's so hot, I don't really feel like going out."

"It's hot here too."

"How's the ocean?"

"Very calm. The moon's out."

"Great. I'll see you tomorrow, I promise. Thanks for calling."

"Good night, dear Marco."

Enza. Now she was on his case too. He was caught in a crossfire with three women. Luckily Marie-Louise was in Paris, and Marco, claiming fear of flying, managed to reduce their encounters to once a month.

Trouble was brewing, however. Marie-Louise was determined to spend her vacation with him. Beatrice had the same intention. Since he'd been with Beatrice on and off for two years now, she held the claim of seniority.

He didn't want to think about it. It made him nervous. And if he felt nervous, he couldn't sleep. For all his forty-five years Marco had managed to avoid all situations that might cause him annoyance or bother even to a slight degree. He insisted on living alone, did everything at the last minute and never planned anything in advance. He couldn't take the stress. If he had to leave for the weekend, he'd work it out tomorrow, depending on the weather and his mood. If he slept badly, for instance, the trip was off. If he slept well, with no disturbing dreams, a couple of newspapers, a relaxing breakfast, some aerobics and he was off.

Saturday afternoons were usually reserved for a trip to his hair stylist, and various errands—the shirtmaker, the jeweler's, an occasional bookshop.

He was beyond filthy rich. Twenty years earlier, when the left-wing government had risen to power, Marco had sold all his considerable real-estate holdings and opened a numbered Swiss bank account. His financial advisors had counseled him so wisely that today nothing short of a nuclear holocaust could affect his wealth.

From year to year other less fortunate people went about their affairs as if caught in a whirlpool. Marco, on the other hand, spent his days serenely in his majestic office on the top floor of a palazzo on Via Montenapoleone. He arrived late in the morning, read a few papers, leafed through a few magazines and then spent ten minutes or so at his personal computer. His PC was loaded with thousands of bits of data: the state of his wardrobe in Milan, in his country villa, in his beach home, in his two other homes; dates of anniversaries, birthdays, name days; statistics on motorboat, auto, and horse races; and the essential statistics on women, subdivided into two major categories—ladies and non-ladies.

His passion—after wristwatches, that is—was high-caliber whores. He frequented several in Milan, Rome, Paris. As for Americans, a special California agency supplied him with pictures and resumes (Special Skills was a fascinating category on these resumes) and Marco gladly paid the fees necessary to fly these women over.

He spent about two hours a day in his office; he had no secretary, he was the sole inhabitant.

Just as he was about to leave, the phone rang.

"It's Alvise Mittaglia."

"How *are* you?"

Skipping over the amenities, Alvise explained what he wanted of him.

"Go to California, talk Rick into coming back—if necessary, kidnap him. That's my job?"

"Precisely. Say you'll do it."

"Sounds like fun. What's in it for me?"

"Name your price."

"I want a valuable watch. Plus an expense account, of course."

"Which watch?"

"I'll leave it up to you, you're a man of taste. Something rare, say late twenties, from one of those antique dealers in London or Geneva."

Marco Fogliani smiled. He would have a marvelous, all expenses paid vacation in California, and then a fine, rare watch waiting for him on his return.

"Well?" Alvise had crossed the fingers on his left hand.

"It's a deal. I'll pull myself out of my Milanese doldrums and go abduct your hot little number. Just what kind of spell has he cast on Ciaccio anyhow?"

"Haven't you ever been really, truly, deeply in love?"

The Big Turk was seated on his throne, formerly a genuine throne—at least according to Gianni Levi, the antique dealer who sold it to him. "You will place your buns exactly where Louis XV had placed his two and a half centuries ago." For this titillation, Ciaccio had forked over 20 million liras. He loved the gilding, the floral intaglios, the authenticity—a real throne. Resting his butt on it provided him a priceless satisfaction. Nevertheless, today, astride his throne, he felt benumbed, paralyzed. Earlier, looking at the drawings on his work table, his eyes had glazed over. Alvise had futilely tried to breathe some semblance of life back into him by showing him a batch of truly stunning original creations. Ciaccio glanced briefly at the drawings, then gazed away. He was encased in a hermetic shell of melancholy. Just for one split second Alvise had caught the glimmer of a sparkle in Ciaccio's eyes. It

50

was when Mara, one of the assistants, had mentioned the name Stanton. She was referring to the photographer Douglas Stanton, but the name was enough to cause a twitch of life in Ciaccio.

At the board room table a while later, Alvise said, "We have to decide on the name for our new men's cologne as soon as possible. The factory's all set to go. The essence was chosen a year ago, the ad campaign's about to get into gear and the distributor's ready and waiting. All we need is a name."

"Tomorrow," Ciaccio murmured. He seemed to deflate even further under the burden of having to say that one word.

"Now," Alvise insisted. "Every day that passes only helps the competition."

He was beginning to get fed up. Yet he couldn't manage without the Big Turk. He had always liked the role of gray eminence, pulling the strings without ever having to face the glare of the spotlight. Ciaccio provided his name and a genius for elegance and taste. Even if they could get along without Ciaccio the person, they couldn't get along without Ciaccio the name. The name by now was part of the magic formula. So, Alvise kept him going, catering to his every whim, no matter how harmful or expensive. Under his breath, Alvise muttered a curse, against whom or what he wasn't even sure. He hoped Marco would be successful in bringing Rick Stanton back to Italy.

"Well, Alvise, do you like it or not?"

"What?"

"For ten minutes now we've been tossing around suggestions and you haven't paid any attention at all."

"Repeat the names."

"Ciaccio, For Men."

"Complicated and ugly."

"Notte."

"Notte. That's all?"

"Yeah."

"Too old-fashioned."

"Wild Horses."

RENZO BARBIERI

"Out of the question. It'll make people think of stables."

"Adventure. In English."

"Possible. But an Italian name would be better. Though Avventura doesn't sound as good, even though it has the secondary meaning of 'Love Affair.' "

The ten men continued throwing out suggestions and Alvise or Ciaccio, mostly Alvise, threw them right back. After a while, Alvise began to suspect that Ciaccio's lethargy might be contagious. This usually inventive group was scraping the barrel with suggestions like Lily-of-the-Valley and Swell Smell. Carletto Magri had just offered the idea: Wet Sweat. Even Ciaccio joined in the general laughter. Acting like his old self he signaled for silence.

"I'm going to call it *Irone*. Just plain *Irone*. "

Whether it was a true inspiration or megalomania in action, everyone heaved a sigh of relief. The boss had come up with the name himself. Alvise studied Ciaccio out of the corner of his eye: Was Ciaccio beginning to recover? He was tempted to call Marco and head him off at the pass.

But, a bit later, when the two of them were alone, Ciaccio fell into a sudden crying jag.

"What's wrong?"

"It would have been great if Rick had been here when we were trying to come up with the name. Without him, success is a mouthful of ashes. Do you know, I was tempted to call it *Rick*?"

In his head, Alvise wished Marco a pleasant flight.

He lingered alone in the board room, thinking about *Irone*. Yes, it would work. Ciaccio had a nose for marketing. He was the one who came up with their trademark—the head of Saladin the Fierce. It was certainly more elegant than Diovisi's two cherries.

"Actually, Lorenzo would much rather have used two testicles," the Empress quipped.

On hearing this Diovisi said, "It was pure autobiography. I prefer cherries to testicles."

Lorenzo Diovisi was in his playroom. When he needed to

52

relax, and the next day's schedule wasn't too demanding, he would spend the evening in his playroom. It had cost him a small fortune to install. A quick glance at it would make you think it was a sort of exercise gym. A more penetrating glance would clear things up—there was no way that the equipment could be used for developing muscles, at least, not the muscles that show when one goes out into the world. Lorenzo called it his playroom, but fantasy-room would be a lot closer to the truth. Needless to say, there were no pinball machines.

There were mirrors everywhere, even on the ceiling. There were leather straps attached to devices rarely seen outside a gynecologist's office. In fact, leather was the general motif of the room. Everything was either leather-lined or had leather straps or at the least leather accessories. It would be difficult to guess how many steers had given up their lives to outfit this one room.

Lorenzo, upon entering the room, just from the smell of the leather, started to get hard. He poured himself some Taittinger champagne as he stripped. Then he put on a leather posing strap—brief in front, nonexistent in back. He was putting on his chrome-studded leather bracelet when he heard a footstep.

"Who's there?"

No answer.

"Is that you, Ruggero?"

Although it was Ruggero, his pre-arranged date for the evening, a tall, massive (in every department), handsome twenty-two-year-old, there still was no answer.

"I said, Who's there?" Lorenzo now was lying face down on a leather mat.

Ruggero, brandishing an authentic whip dating back to the days of the Spanish Inquisition, stepped out into the light. He wore enough leather on his various appendages to establish him as the King of Leather.

Seeing him, Lorenzo gasped. "Oh no. Please, no. Anything but that."

In the interests of discretion, let us draw a curtain—leather-

53

lined, if you will—across this scene of domestic happiness and wish the participants a pleasant evening of fun and entertainment.

Chapter 5

"We will be landing at Los Angeles International Airport in fifteen minutes. Please extinguish all smoking materials and make sure your seatbelts are properly fastened. We will be landing at approximately 6:45 P.M. The temperature in Los Angeles is 82 degrees. We hope you've had a pleasant trip. We thank you for flying Pan Am and we hope you will fly again with us in the future. Thank you."

He must be a new pilot, thought Marco, as the intercom switched off. He forgot all about warning us to stay in our seats until the plane taxis to a complete stop. Or maybe he said it before and I was too lost in my daydream to notice. Maybe I'm in jet lag and don't even know it. He stretched his arms up as high as his seatbelt would permit and groaned at the effort. He couldn't wait to get off the plane and walk again.

Bob Manley was waiting for him at the Pinkerton offices. Did he ever go home? Maybe he slept in his office. And he seemed tied to the office as well—Marco could not get him to leave the office to accompany him to see Rick Stanton.

"I've spoken to the kid. He refuses to meet with me. But the evening you arrive, he'll be at a party and I've got an invitation for you. The host said he'd be privileged to meet the right-hand man of Italy's great Ciaccio Irone."

"I'm not Ciaccio's right-hand man," Marco replied. "I'm not even on his staff. I'm a businessman and I'm a friend of Alvise Mittaglia. It's him I'm doing this favor for."

"I understand."

"Say, I hope this isn't an all-gay party." It's not that Marco was in any way anti-gay that made him ask this question. It was just that a party without even the possibility of a little discreet cruising did not hold out much promise for a great evening on the town.

"Don't worry. There'll be plenty of beautiful women there too."

"Whores?" Marco asked, his eyes beginning to sparkle.

"Excuse me. I thought you said . . . "

"Whores. I did."

"Not that I know of. Mostly wives and daughters of businessmen. Of course there's always a handful of starlets at parties like this. You never know. You'll have to do your own research."

Marco certainly wasn't interested in the wives and daughters. As for the starlets, his experience had led him to avoid them as much as possible. No matter how ready and willing they were— and some were extremely so—they were, in his experience, simply not able. No, he liked the real pros, those who would charge $2000 plus airfare for a night, those who looked like *Playboy* centerfolds, but knew their business outside and in, so to speak; experts in the *art* of sex.

He had been told by Manley that he would feel right at home. "What do you mean by that?"

"The host is an Italo-American and he's celebrating the eightieth anniversary of his family's arriving in this country."

Though most of the help—waiters, kitchen staff—were either black or Hispanic, they were all dressed in traditional Italian peasant clothes. The traditional costumes only added to the slightly freaky atmosphere. The musicians—seven old geezers imported from New York's Little Italy—did have an air of authenticity at least, as they wheezed out Neapolitan and Sicilian tunes on their ancient accordions and mandolins.

Plastic almond blossoms (made in Taiwan) were handed out as well as (California) oranges with the date 1905 stamped on them—the year Frank Danello's great-grandfather arrived in New York.

The cake itself was eye-catching. Standing a full ten feet high, it was a replica of Mount Etna in full eruption—marzipan-based, with whipped cream for the snow. The lava in rich chocolate, flowed into the base of a nougat sea, which was of course dotted with candy boats.

By ten the party was in full swing. The driveway was lined on both sides and down the hill with Bentleys, Rolls-Royces and hired limos. The guest list was a classy one, everyone dressed to the teeth, the men in evening wear, the women in the most fashionable dresses and dripping with jewelry.

A herd of goons was discreetly scattered among the paths and shrubbery to keep matters under control.

Frank and his wife Rosy personally welcomed every guest. Rosy Danello was a plump little woman who had hit the pasta much too often over the years. She wore a green evening gown that flowed around her. Although clearly expensive, because of her shape, it seemed like someone had draped a green gunny sack around her and let it be that. Around her neck, however, she wore a fabulous ruby necklace which Marco, upon kissing her hand in the old style upon introduction, estimated to be at the least a $200,000 bagatelle.

"They tell me you work with Ciaccio Irone," she suggested.

"I'm only a friend."

"I wish he were here at the party tonight," she said, moving her eyes onto the next guests, dismissing a mere friend of Irone's as clearly used goods.

The goon who was imitating a footman announced, "Senator and Mrs. Deseret of Utah."

This was Marco's cue to move it along and he did so. He bumped into a handsome man in his thirties who smiled at him beatifically. Marco introduced himself.

"My name's Priya," the other said.

"How unusual," Marco said. Only one name. Hm. "Is that by any chance Portuguese?"

"Sanskrit," was the reply.

"Oh," said Marco, taken aback.

"It means 'beloved.' "

"Excuse me. I think I see an old friend," Marco lied.

By midnight, Rick Stanton had yet to show up. Marco had just finished dancing a tarantella with a middle-aged woman with very young breasts and buttocks.

"You're the second nicest Italian male I've ever met," she said in parting.

Marco graciously thanked her and walked away, wondering who number one was. Vito Genovese? Tony Bennett?

Most of the guests were indeed businessmen and their families, as Manley had said. There was an occasional senator or sportswriter to lend a little class, but with the exception of a handful of pitifully pretty starlets, not a serious pro in the house. He moved from room to room overhearing snatches of conversations.

"Do you believe Betty is still a virgin?"

"Who wants to look like Joan Collins, for gosh sakes!"

"The girls just adore Camp Sunshine."

"You must meet my guru."

"Do bananas give you diarrhea too?"

"When do you think they'll cut the cake?"

"You pay rent? I thought only poor people pay rent."

Bored, with nothing better to do, Marco found himself count-ing the number of people he saw chewing gum. He found himself in the garden and sat down on a marble bench—or a sarcophagus, it was a little hard to tell.

From behind him, there was a rustle and then a single American word of greeting, "Hi."

Rick Stanton's splendid, tanned face emerged from behind the fronds. "I bet you're the Italian who wants to meet me."

"You guessed it."

Rick sat down next to him. He held a glass filled with a li-quid that was blood red.

"Is that blood you're drinking?"

"No, my own concoction, mostly grenadine."

"How did you know I was the Italian looking for you?"

"You certainly aren't American. The giveaway is, you know how to dress. Americans are always screwing it up. Especially when they think everything 'matches.' That's when everything is some shade of green, say. They ought to hand out sunglasses. It's enough to make you lose faith in human decency."

"While we're on the subject of human decency," Marco in-terrupted, "I'd like to know why you walked out on Ciaccio without even saying goodbye."

"If I had tried to say a personal goodbye, he would have done everything to talk me out of it."

"You seemed to care for him. Don't you any more?"

As soon as the words came out, Marco wanted to retrieve them. They sounded mawkish and silly to his ears. He tried a dif-ferent tack.

"How much were you paid to leave Italy?"

Rick made a half-hearted attempt to look offended, but then laughed in spite of himself. He decided to put his cards on the table.

"O.K. Here's the truth. This guy I didn't know from Adam came to me. Maybe he was some competitor of Ciaccio's. You would know more about these things. Anyhow, he says, 'There's a plane leaving for New York at noon tomorrow. This is to make sure you're on it.' He hands me a check—a six-figure check."

"Liras!"

"Get real. Dollars."

"Since we're putting our cards on the table, let me say, I'm prepared to make you a counter offer. How much do you want to come back to Ciaccio?"

"You won't believe me, but money isn't the issue."

"You just bragged about a six-figure sum and now you tell me money isn't the issue."

"It's not the important, the fundamental issue."

"You've stopped liking gay sex."

"Men, women—it's all the same to me. That's true. So long as I feel loved."

"So you want to stay in America?" Marco was baffled. Once he realized a money offer, no matter how large, wouldn't do the trick, he was stymied.

"No, I prefer Italy. I like the people, the climate, the lifestyle—everything. Keep this under your hat, but, confidentially, I feel a real affection for Ciaccio."

"I give up. Explain to me then why you won't come back."

"Look at it from my point of view. As a model, what have I got to look forward to? Maybe a few more years, tops. The new crop is already arriving. Selling my ass is a drag. I'm essentially very lazy, and also monogamous. I have trouble getting used to new lovers. What I long for is security, a solid income, a luxurious life. Anyone who can guarantee me all that can have me. And I'll be faithful in the bargain."

"If I understand you correctly, you want something like a lifetime annuity."

"More than that. I have social ambitions as well. I want to be high up on the social ladder as well. In short, I want to make what you people call 'a good marriage.' "

"If you were a woman, Ciaccio would be an ideal catch. Since Ciaccio is genitally, uh legally, a man . . . "

There was a pause as a black-clad black waiter passed silently by. Rick plucked a drink from the tray.

"Here. You look like you need it. I'll stick with my grenadine. Here they only serve hard liquor, which is hell on the complexion."

Marco, at a loss for words, sipped at his drink.

Rick, continuing, said, "Ciaccio only has to marry me and I'll come back."

"Ah, now I understand. All of Bel Reame attends a grand wedding. Some lady pope of the fashion world officiates. A thousand guests . . . "

"You don't begin to understand, if that's what you think," Rick said. "I'm not talking about some phony gay marriage. I want to become—legally—a member of the Irone family."

Trying not to look too dense, Marco said, "How do you expect to do that?"

"By marrying Ciaccio's sister."

"What?"

"You heard me, Alvise. That son-of-a-bitch will return only if Ciaccio lets him marry his sister."

"Is he in love with Sabina?" Alvise asked.

"As it turns out, Rick hardly knows her. Whatever else this kid is, he's not stupid. He's figured out all the angles. He wants an established base—the Irone family. He even stipulated what sums of money he would want for alimony if there's a divorce."

"Holy mother of God!"

"Listen, I can't talk too long, I'm calling from the party. I'm now right in the upholstered study of someone named Frank Danello."

Flustered, Alvise said, "Where does this Danello come in to the picture?"

"Forget I mentioned him. Anyway, now you understand what Rick wants in exchange for returning to Ciaccio?"

"It's totally absurd. You've met Sabina. She's young, intelligent, attractive, she's got a degree in languages. And, one other point, she's also engaged—to a wealthy industrialist. She adores her brother, but I don't think she's about to jeopardize her entire future just so 'Big Jim' can return to Ciaccio's waiting sheets."

"As the Americans say, the ball's in your court. As far as I'm concerned, I've completed my assignment. I hope the watch you picked out for me is a beauty."

"Wait . . . What if we kidnapped him? You could rent a private plane . . . No, forget it. I'll talk to Ciaccio. He'll have to decide."

Marco hung up. With his "job" done, now all he had to think about was having a good time. He had Rick's phone number and address. He wondered if Ciaccio—or Sabina—would agree to the marriage.

Marco's eyes were caught by a statuesque blond woman, somewhere in her late twenties. She was talking to Rossano Valverde, the famous Italian actor of the thirties who, with the aid of a delicate-handed plastic surgeon, had aged remarkably well. He had recently come into a new wave of success in America, playing a kind of Cesar Romero type in a tawdry late night soap opera. All of a sudden he was a sex symbol again.

The blonde was very much to Marco's taste—smooth, leggy, big-breasted. She could have stepped out of *Playboy* (no staple).

He maneuvered toward her. All three smiled at each other. And then she was gone. Poor Marco after looking everywhere for her found himself stuck with Valverde and his gleaming smile. Valverde pulled up a chair, gave a little groan and sat down. "How do you like California?"

Marco replied, "All I know of it actually, is this house."

Valverde said, "That's the same with me. All I ever see is the inside of hotels or studios or producers' offices or, to be perfectly frank, beauty parlors. I wonder what they're called now. They called them beauty parlors in my heyday. But then we didn't even have TV."

Marco was amused by the actor's candor.

"Do I look tan? It's from a lamp. You like my silver hair. See, it's a toupee. Then there's the facelift, the caps, the contact lenses.

62

I'm not kidding when I say that in the morning when I look in the mirror I don't recognize me."

Aha. The blonde had reappeared. She was standing over in a corner in a sort of amorous huddle with a handsome young man. "I have an idea," Marco said. Indicating the blonde, he said, "Why don't the three of us go out and discover L.A. together."

"You really don't know L.A., do you? It's the most dangerous city at night. Murders, rapes, robberies. L.A. is a city made up of a lot of little cities—all of them dangerous—especially on foot."

To Marco's dismay, the handsome guy the blonde had been talking to had disappeared and now was returning carrying her wrap. Another lost opportunity.

Marco stood up.

"Where are you going?" Valverde asked.

"To find a hooker," Marco replied impulsively.

"You won't find any."

"Don't tell me L.A. is the only city in the world without prostitutes."

"More than enough. But there are no streetwalkers because L.A. is the only city in the world without sidewalks. Nobody walks. Everybody drives. Of course there are prostitutes, all kinds. Come on, we'll go and visit Mr. Amodio. He's a *paisan*."

"Mr. Amodio's salon is unique as far as I know. It's got a gym and a sauna, and God knows how many other amenities. But it's not famous for that. It's a land of toys and fantasies, a utopia for the rich. Accepting all major credit cards. Ask for it. They have it. I'm not kidding. You'll see soon enough," Valverde explained in the cab. They finally arrived in Beverly Hills. They drove through a large gateway onto Rodeo Drive. The cab stopped by an elevator.

As Marco reached for the door, Valverde checked him. "You don't have to get out. The elevator will take us to the salon. It's 100 feet below street level."

Two men in tuxedos appeared and checked Valverde's ID and

Marco's passport.

"They've got guns," Marco observed.

"A precaution. The important people who visit here don't want any unpleasant surprises."

They had descended to the bottom. They walked down a long corridor lit by quartz lamps. "Walk slowly and you'll get a nice tan," Valverde commented.

Uniformed women replaced the armed guards. They wore green miniskirts and green blouses embroidered with a big *A* on their breasts. Shades of *The Scarlet Letter*, Marco thought, smiling to himself. Each door had a sign in neon above it. Depilator, Reading Room, Cinema, Aerosol . . . etc.

Valverde enjoyed playing guide. "If you have some secret desire, no matter how 'forbidden,' this is the place to satisfy it. Just ask and pay." They were passing the Greek Room, the Roman Room, California Champagne Room, the Wild West Room . . .

They entered another corridor. This one had lots of doors as well but no signs. "This is where you can get inventive," Valverde said.

They entered a Massage Room.

"Together?" asked the woman, nonplussed.

"No."

She led them to a smaller room, where what light there was was faintly blue. Background music, mostly played on lutes, it seemed. Incense from a small brazier. The bed, made of rushes, had a dragon embroidered on the sheet.

The woman, lying very naked on the bed, introduced herself. "Hi, my name's Brenda."

She got up and started helping Marco to undress. "Do you want a relaxing massage or a therapeutic one?"

Silently he lay belly-down on the bed.

"Very well, sir. I know a special cream to activate your circulation."

She unscrewed the top of a jar lying nearby.

64

Then she straddled him, and massaged him actively, almost fiercely, periodically her swinging breasts rubbing against parts of his back. The cream spread heat across his back.

"Please turn over on your back now."

He turned over. Her breasts were very large but in proportion to her frame. She proceeded to massage every part of the front of him, again hitting up against him from time to time with her breasts. Finally she got around to his groin. She anointed his penis, his testicles.

"Do you need complete relaxation?" she asked. "Would you prefer one of my colleagues? Black or white?"

"I think you'll do fine," he said. He put a hand on her head and guided it toward the head of his cock.

Chapter 6

*D*iana Rau was having one of those days that start out full of promise. At nine A.M., she was awakened by a florist delivering a splendid bouquet of roses from Kao, who at that moment was in Australia. She arranged the roses in a huge silver vase and went dreamily back to sleep. She attributed her good looks and their staying power to her dictum: Never let them wake you up until you're all slept out. At noon, she got up, bathed and spent a while admiring her naked body in a full-length mirror. She decided she was just as beautiful now as she was when she was 18.

At two P.M. sharp she called Pier Damiano and broke off with him. He had not made a scene, had not even asked for severance pay. For all she knew, he already had someone else lined up. At any rate, he gave the impression that he was as disturbed as if his hair stylist called to cancel an appointment.

It was two-thirty P.M. Monday afternoon, and Diana was feeling great about herself. She was beautiful, and she was on the verge of hooking her very own billionaire.

The phone rang. Diana looked at her Audemars Pigeut wristwatch and wondered, If all good things come in threes . . .

"Hi, this is Fuxia, Fuxia Taylor. I'm a friend of your niece, Inna."

"I remember you very well," Diana said coldly.

Fuxia, was the American tramp whom Inna palled around with. She had told Diana that she'd been named after the fuchsia.

"Inna's sick, very sick. Could you come over here right away?"

Fuxia, for a change, didn't sound in the least bit stoned. From her tone of voice Diana could tell she wasn't joking. All at once, Diana could feel her day crumbling around her.

Diana really loved Inna, her sister Cora's only child. In Inna, Diana could see herself younger, at the start of her career, eager and willing to work hard to get somewhere. Physically they were different types. Inna was softer and sexier, Diana more classy and aggressive.

But times had changed. When Diana was starting out, the greatest risk she had run was selling her body cheap, or worse yet, to the wrong purchaser. Today, the field in one sense was smaller, though fashion journals and houses had proliferated; even with the dominance of the Italian Style in the international market, though the demand for flesh had grown, so had the huge influx of American Barbies and Big Jims. The American girls, tall, blonde, with perfect skin, came flocking in and inundated the agencies with their glossies. The Italian girls had less and less space for maneuvering, and it was getting more and more difficult to use the traditional tool of sex, since now more than three quarters of the big fashion houses were run by gay males.

And then there were the more traditional pitfalls as well: alcohol, drugs, especially cocaine, which was omnipresent in the fashion world; there were the vultures, the profiteers, the photographers, the con men, with their Kleenex approach to women.

Diana felt too upset to drive. She hailed a cab and gave the address. It was the Princess Clothilde Hostel. Practically all the American models lived here, and the agencies knew it. It had been nicknamed the Princess Clithilde. Inna wanted to be independent so she roomed there with Fuxia, rather than economizing and staying with her aunt.

Fuxia was nervously pacing.

"What happened?"

"Ask the doctor. He'll tell you."

"I want to hear your version."

Fuxia led her over to the window. This was the first time Diana had seen her sober and without any makeup. With her red hair and enormous green eyes, she was remarkably beautiful.

"We were in bed with two guys," Fuxia explained. "We had lots of whiskey and lots of coke, believe me, lots. Anyhow, Inna seemed fine this morning when they left, but she nodded off and her breathing sounded so odd, I tried to wake her. I couldn't. I called the doctor. He says it's the coke. Inna's still in the coma."

"He called it a coma?" cried Diana. She ran into the bedroom.

The doctor was youngish, no older than forty, with very thick glasses. He was looking clearly worried. He gazed at Diana, disapprovingly.

"Are you her mother?"

"I'm her aunt."

"The girl should be taken to a hospital and kept under close observation. I've arranged to have her taken to Niguarda."

"We'll take her to Santa Tecla Clinic," Diana said decisively, also letting the doctor know that money was no obstacle in caring for her niece. She looked down at Inna's still body lying in the middle of the king-size bed. She sighed. Inna seemed so young, so defenseless.

There was no trace left of the preceding evening's activities— the bed's sheets were fresh, there were no drugs or bottles in sight. Diana thanked Fuxia for having had the foresight to take care of all that before the doctor arrived.

The ambulance arrived and two hefty men strapped Inna onto a gurney and started carrying her down. Feeling the need to blow off some steam, Diana turned on Fuxia and said, "When she recovers she'll live with me. I don't want her seeing hide nor hair of you ever again. I'll have someone come for her things."

Fuxia started to cry soundlessly, the tears running down her cheeks. "I love Inna like a sister," she cried. "Maybe more, I don't know. But you don't know Inna the way I do. Her appetite for sex—men, women—it doesn't matter. She's voracious. She would brag to me about her exploits. It used to eat me up. The orgies . . . "

"Stop it!" Diana screamed. "I don't want to hear any more of this filth. Even if you aren't to blame for her wild behavior, I still want her to come live with me when she gets better," Diana concluded, ignoring Fuxia's tears.

With the (expensive) right equipment and the (expensive) proper care, it seemed almost miraculously soon that the doctors and attendants at Santa Tecla were about to break through to Inna and to get her out of her coma-like stupor.

Dr. Zerli, the head physician explained in an uncharacteristic fit of humility, "I wouldn't exactly call it a coma. It was sort of a catalepsy. It's not uncommon among people who overdo their cocaine."

Diana, nevertheless, was very grateful. "You can send all her bills to me," she said. He assured Diana there would be time for that when Inna was well and ready to be checked out.

After he left, Diana sat in Inna's room brooding. She was not one to avoid a hard truth and the hard truth of the matter here was that Fuxia was probably right. Diana cast her mind back over previous stories, experiences at parties, whispers among her friends. Was it true? Was Inna's appetite for sex of any and all kinds so voracious? It was a measure of how Diana looked at the world that her first thought was not about the toll this might take on Inna psychologically, but what effect it would have on Inna's career prospects.

Diana Rau, the most famous Italian fashion model of her day, never had such problems. Sex was simply a tool, used only to advance her career. Inna, on the other hand, seemed a true slave to her passion.

Alvise Mittaglia was stumped. There was no way he could avoid telling Ciaccio the conditions stipulated by Rick; then again, he couldn't find the right way to approach the subject. With an air of abandoning all hope, he finally just blurted it out any which way and stood there waiting for the dust to settle.

"He wants to get married?" Ciaccio asked.

Alvise couldn't believe his ears. The sound made by Ciaccio sounded like a cry of triumph.

"Is that all he wants? Ah, the dear, sweet, wonderful, beautiful, *monogamous* boy! That's what he shall have. In spades. It will be the most beautiful wedding Bel Reame has ever seen."

In a wee small voice, realizing Ciaccio hadn't quite grasped the entire proposition as yet, Alvise said, "Hold on. I'm not quite sure you understand what Rick means by a wedding. He wants a legal marriage contract and a full- blown *real* church wedding." Alvise realized how difficult it was in the fashion world to get the concept of *real* across.

Still not entirely on top of the situation, Ciaccio retorted, "But I'm a man!" and then looked around in a funny way, as if there might be someone present to dispute the fact. "I mean, legally. Wait a minute. I'm not going to Casablanca for any of those funny operations they perform down there." Alvise wasn't sure whether 'down there' referred to Casablanca or to Ciaccio's genitalia.

"No, no. Nothing like that."

"I like men, but I'm a man too. Anything else would be unnatural, if you know what I mean."

"No, Rick has very shrewdly come up with his own solution

71

to the problem."

"It had better be good. Not like some of those countries these days that have gay marriages and lesbian priests and stuff."

"No. Much more conventional than that. Rick wants to marry Sabina."

"Sabina. How did she enter the picture? Is he in love with her?"

"I seriously doubt it. No, it's all part of his elaborate scheme. Rick has something very different in mind. By marrying her, he wouldn't take on the name Irone, but he'd come close enough, he'd be a member of the family. He'd be Sabina's husband only on paper, he'd be your husband in reality."

Even though it entailed the use of the word *reality*, this time Alvise felt reasonably sure he had conveyed the full import of Rick's elaborate yet reasonably straight-forward scheme. He had known Ciaccio for a half a lifetime and thought he knew him well. He was sure Ciaccio would not go for it. He cared too much for his sister. He wouldn't sell her down the river, lock, stock, and wedding finger, all for a stud, no matter how sensationally attractive.

"What a wonderful idea! What a genius of an idea!"

Alvise picked at the wax in his left ear. It had a tendency to pile up in there. Surely he hadn't heard right. "Huh," he said, baffled.

"Don't ever let anyone tell you Rick isn't smart. It's so simple, so elegant. Rick will marry Sabina but he'll live with me. Now that's what I call love!"

Alvise sat there in his armchair, astonished. Ciaccio was rattling on, gushing with his new-found happiness. "Sabina won't say no. She enjoys her lifestyle much too much and it's all because of Irone Fashions she can live like that. She loves me, she'll want to see me happy. Besides, she likes Rick. She met him a few times and it was apparent they hit if off together."

Fishing for objections like a drowning man for a lifeline, Alvise said, "And you're not jealous?"

"Don't be silly. Of my own sister? What a menage à trois we'll

72

be, like Huey, Dewey and Louie. Oh I'm so happy!" We'll honey-moon in Bora Bora!"

The only real—there was that concept again—obstacle to all this was Sabina's fiance, an ex-publisher who had become a paper manufacturer. Sabina had fallen in love with him. Here was a job for Alvise.

Curtly, imperiously, Ciaccio ordered, "Find his weak spot and send him packing. Do it in such a way so that he's the one who leaves Sabina."

"I don't see how . . . " Alvise started.

"Just do it."

Chapter 7

*E*verybody has some purely physical craving, something so dark and base hidden deep within us that we dare not reveal it even to those closest to us, certainly not a lover or spouse. With some people it entails unusual acts of sex with strangers, often of a physically violent sort; for some, it can be as seemingly innocent as stuffing one's face with pastries and watching television for hours on end. We all have something to hide. This was as true of Sabina's fiancé, Carlo Venanzi, head of Robotti Paper, Inc., as it is for the rest of us.

Carlo's taxi pulled to a stop in front of number two Via Caronia, a sad, down-at-the-heels neighborhood on the outskirts of Milan. As he stepped out of the taxi, it was instantly apparent that this was not his element. He was wearing a gray Prince of Wales suit. In one hand he carried an attache case (Hermès), in the other a newspaper *(The Wall Street Journal).*

As the taxi pulled away, neither the driver nor Venanzi was aware that it had been followed by the green Giulietta now passing it and turning the corner before coming to a stop. There were three men in the Giulietta—the driver, a young man with a Nikon around his neck who gave off an air of knowing a lot about cameras, at least under these odd circumstances, and our old friend Alvise Mittaglia.

Blackmail, like many a more respectable business, is nevertheless a business. And as is often true in business, if you want something to be done right, make sure you yourself are in charge. This was the thinking behind Alvise's presence in the Giulietta.

They waited a couple of discretionary minutes and then jumped out of the car and headed toward the building they had watched Venanzi enter.

The concierge was a middle-aged woman busy reading the daily comics. They asked here where Venanzi had gone, describing him in detail.

"Lots of people come through here," she said laconically.

Alvise held up a 10,000 lire note.

"Stairway A, fifth floor. Signora Allodi," she said as the note disappeared with magical speed into her capacious bosom.

"Who is she?"

"A tenant."

Another 10,000.

She was getting a little nervous. "Are you from the police?"

"Since when have the police become so generous?"

"Signora Allodi has a daughter."

"Well?"

Another 10,000.

"The little girl has many uncles. Well, maybe not so many, but the ones she has are devoted. And they all seem to be quite well off financially." The concierge lowered her guard as well as her paper. The chance for gossip was irresistible. "Signora Allodi is always complaining how poor she is, but she lives like someone out of the movies. She takes expensive vacations, and last year she was sporting a mink, a real mink coat. Good stuff."

"Let's go," said the photographer.

"There's no rush. This uncle usually stays for a good hour." She was quite prepared to chat by now, without the fuelling of 10,000 lira notes.

They took the ancient rickety elevator up to the fifth floor. There were two doors. They knocked on the one that had the nameplate with Allodi on it.

"Who is it?" a female voice called out.

"Flowers."

The door was opened. Signora Allodi was wearing a suit of a bright pink velvet that did nothing for any one of her irregular features. She started to slam the door when she saw there were three men and no flowers. They all three dashed into the foyer and closed the door behind them. The driver immobilized her, his hand over her mouth. He whispered, "If you let out even a peep, I'll bash your head in for you."

The other two entered the parlor, whose floor was shiny with wax.

From an ashtray by the one armchair, wreaths of smoke were curling up from an incompletely put-out cigarette. While the photographer set up his equipment, Alvise placed his ear flush against the door to the bedroom. After a bit, he crouched and peered through the keyhole.

He was able to get quite a view of the bedroom from his small peephole. It was a child's bedroom, all in pink. There was a single bed with Snoopy sheets. The small table seemed to be covered with comics and children's picture books. There was a blackboard in the corner and toys, mostly stuffed animals, seemed to be scattered everywhere. On the wall above the bed was a standard Madonna and Child, the Holy Infant all smiles. Venanzi was standing over near the blackboard, dressed as he was when he entered the building.

The little girl wore a flowery little frock with a full skirt, black patent leather shoes and white bobbysox. She had been drawing something on the blackboard. Now she turned and smiled at Venanzi.

She looked to be all of twelve, thirteen at the most. Her face was still swathed in baby fat. Her body, however, was a bit more developed than one might expect. Her breasts were decidedly present and her legs, on second examination, seemed quite well developed.

Alvise began to think that he'd made a blunder. What greeted his eye was to all intents and purposes a visit to a girl by her uncle. Then the little girl stepped aside. She had drawn on the blackboard an extremely accurate picture. As Alvise said later, "That was no phallic symbol, that was *it*."

"Aren't I a good girl, Uncle?"

Sitting down on the bed, he slapped his knees and said, "Come sit here, *cara*."

"What game do you want to play today, Uncle?" the little girl asked.

Alvise could barely hear her suggestions, but Venanzi kept shaking his head no at her, suggesting to Alvise that they were long-time playmates and had quite a repertory of games.

"How about the uncle who takes his niece to bed because she's scared of thunder?"

"No."

"How about the teacher who punishes the pupil for not doing her homework?"

"Silvana! We played that last time."

"Little Red Riding Hood and the Wolf?"

"No."

The little girl frowned, her expression suddenly turning sour and older as she said, "Make up your mind and fuck me already. I'm getting bored."

Alvise was rather enjoying himself, so much so he had to stifle a laugh. That would louse things up nicely. So, Venanzi, so proper, so gray-suited and correct in his social life, had a flaw. He liked nymphets. Of all the possibilities, all in all, that wasn't very

78

zi froze in position as if playing a game of statues. Correction: there was some movement—his cock went from very hard to limp and flaccid in a remarkably short space of time. Before Venanzi could do anything as basic as reach for his pants, the invaders had already pulled up stakes and left.

Two days later, Sabina received an anonymous envelope filled with interesting and revealing pictures.

She called Venanzi and told him about the photos.

"This is a trick of Ciaccio's," Venanzi screamed over the phone. "I recognized his partner, that asshole Mittaglia."

"And while we're on the subject of recognition, *I* recognized *you* in the photos."

"Darling, be reasonable. It was just a harmless peccadillo, certainly not worth getting upset over."

"Children! Of all things. I could understand other men, even German Shepherds; but children! If we got married and had kids, what's to stop you from doing it with our *own* children?"

Venanzi winced. "That's hitting below the belt, Sabina. That's disgusting. You're talking about incest. This is just pedophilia. Be reasonable."

Sabina hung up. On the one hand she felt relief that the affair was over. On the other, she resented her brother's underhanded intervention, for she was sure it was his doing. Sabina knew something was in the air. Ciaccio was making more efforts to spend time with her. And he was so overtly affectionate and warm, she had become suspicious. Then, also, there were all these casual references to Rick Stanton. There was even a hint in the air that she might be interested in a sort of marriage—was that possible?—to Rick. Whose crazy idea was that one? She had a lot to figure out.

Only one thought was crystal clear in her mind: Ciaccio had been financially helpful in setting up Ranetti in the past and seemed to be talking that way about Rick now. If he was going to be a goose who laid golden eggs, she expected the goose to lay more for his sister than he would for a lover.

80

She sat down at the table, pulled over a pad and pencil and started idly making a shopping list. Villa, yacht, airplane . . .

Chapter 8

*F*ilippo Ranetti was in conference in his office with two Americans.

The phone rang. "Damn," he said to himself. "Excuse me a moment," he said to the Americans.

It was Dindino, his lover, his own precious treasure.

"I thought I told you not to call me at the office."

"I wouldn't if it weren't so serious."

"We'll talk about it later. I'll be home at the usual time for dinner."

"That's too late, I need you right now."

The Empress hung up. He buzzed his secretary. "I thought I told you no calls."

"I'm sorry. It was Dindino and he sounded desperate."

"No calls when I'm in conference. Is that understood?"

"Yes, sir."

Turning back to the two Americans, he asked in his halting Berlitz English, "Where were we?"

"We were talking about the silver process."

"Oh, yes." The reference was to a new process that would make furs virtually indestructible. It would be the fashion find of the decade. Talk about an original idea! The Americans picked up a book of sketches and studied them. Trust Ranetti. His fashion concepts were unique, one of a kind originals.

"And you want exclusive rights for all of North America?"

"Yes."

"Fine. I think we can sew up a deal in no time."

Like everyone else in Bel Reame, whatever kind of dalliance or foolish indulgence one had in one's private life, one never let it spill over into one's business affairs. This was true of all of Bel Reame. If the Marquis de Sade seemed to be the patron saint of their private lives, their professional saint was Machiavelli. Most of the people in the fashion world had risen from the lowest depths of poverty and much of their international success was based on the desire—the need—to be absolutely ruthless in business.

The Empress was typical in many ways. He was born in Liguria, of a poor family. At fifteen, he had gone to work as a sort of messenger for a furrier. He was not dumb. He soon realized that unless he got lucky, he had few prospects between his penniless adolescence and his pinchbeck retirement at sixty.

He found men more generous to him than women, they had more money to spend on him and their vices. So he supplemented his meager income by hustling. Everything he made went into a bank account. He had developed a secret wish to open his own small fur store.

Then fate stepped in. A rich Milanese (electric appliances) fell in love with him and took him back to Milan. He was generous and showed Filippo his first glimpses of a life where money was not a consideration. Not a month after the industrialist bankrolled Filippo in his own small workshop, through a combination of stress and overwork he died of a massive heart attack.

During a display at a fashion fair, Filippo bumped into Ciaccio and for both it was love at first sight. Like all first loves, from a dispassionate distance their affair seemed maudlin and silly. But not of course to them. They wrote poems to and for each other every day, poems of an awfulness that only deep love could forgive. Ciaccio was especially fond of the sonnet form. Since until then his writing ability had been confined to checks, he secretly hired a poor student to write the sonnets for him. It was Ciaccio's biggest fear that Ranetti would discover that they were ghostwritten.

It was a happy season for the Empress. He was young, loved and in love, and, best of all, launched in society. Within a year, Irone's clientele had become Ranetti's too.

Women who should have known better would say things like:

"I don't understand it, but every time I put on my Ranetti fur I become wildly horny."

Or: "I wore my Ranetti fur to go shopping in the other day. What a trip! I was totally naked underneath. By the time I got home I was so horny I attacked my husband—it was the first time we'd had sex in more than five years. He kept saying, 'Elsa, what's the matter?'"

Filippo had encouraged the rumors (which he started in the first place) that his furs acted as aphrodisiacs. His sales skyrocketed.

Everything was going great for Ranetti until Rick Stanton appeared on the scene. Suddenly he was 86'd from Ciaccio's crowd. If the blow fell harder on his ego than on his heart, well, things happen like that and a hurt ego can also cause a lot of pain.

Anyhow, by the time of the great breakup, Ranetti's reputation had been made. He was part of the fashion establishment. The big difference was that now he was in such a powerful position that he found himself surrounded by handsome young male proteges, more than happy to curry his favor. It's a shorter trip, he found out, from Galatea to Pygmalion than one would suppose.

He met Dindino one night at Versace's. He had never seen any man so beautiful, tall and muscular, very blond, deep blue eyes. Ranetti couldn't take his eyes off Dindino. His companion that evening, Fiffa Comitoni, the fashion writer, noticing what was going on, leaned over to Ranetti and whispered, "You get bloodshot if you don't blink." So it was that noticeable.

Ranetti made an effort to look somewhere else.

"Besides," Fiffa added, "he's already taken."

"By someone in our crowd?"

"No, an architect. Made a bundle building villas in Sardinia."

"As long as he's not one of us," Filippo answered, meaning of course, anyone in the Milan fashion world. This is the closest Bel Reame came to *noblesse oblige.*

In very short order, Ranetti pounced. Dindino was won over, Teo the architect threw a tantrum made up mostly of possessive jealousy, and in no time flat Dindino had moved out from Teo and in with Ranetti.

In the tradition he himself had been a part of, Filippo put Dindino to work in his workshop for two reasons: 1) to keep him busy and 2) to teach him a trade. From the start Dindino showed evidence of possessing a keen eye and refined taste.

Aside from the obvious allurements, money brings, along with its perks and privileges, power. Although Ranetti had become enormously wealthy, so much so that he had more than enough to last him the rest of a long and lavish lifetime, he still drove himself as hard as ever. It was the feeling of power over others that spurred him on now, that and the still-fresh memories of growing up poor.

After the conference with the Americans had ended, the Empress leaned back in his office chair and heaved a self-satisfied sigh. How *easy* it was to be ruthless, it hardly took any effort.

He arrived home, placatory bouquet of jonquils in hand, to be greeted by Sadong, the Thai major domo at the door. Sadong merely pointed to the bedroom Ranetti shared with Dindino and shook his head sadly.

Dindino was sprawled across the bed, weeping steadily, his shoulders rising and falling in rhythm to his sobs.

"I'm here, baby . . . I'm home."

"Don't try and suck up to me now. You hung up on me when I really needed you."

Leaning over, Filippo caressed Dindino's silky shoulders, he stroked Dindino's silky hair.

"You know I couldn't come sooner. I was working, in an important conference. But, now I'm home, I'm all yours. How can I help, baby? What's wrong?"

"You . . . I . . . Something dreadful happened."

Ranetti was stroking Dindino's hair. He was also beginning to get a hardon.

"Tell me everything. It can't be all that terrible."

"I was driving my Honda along Corso Venezia."

"What were you doing out there?" the Empress asked in a slight fit of suspicious jealousy.

"I was just out for a spin."

"And then what?" Ranetti crossed his legs.

"I was stopped at a light. A Porsche pulled up next to me and of all people Teo got out. Between him and his chauffeur they took my Honda, my gold chain and my Rolex. It all happened so fast the light hadn't even changed."

"Didn't you try and defend yourself at all? You're not exactly a weakling," Ranetti said as he stroked Dindino's biceps.

"It was all too sudden. I was scared."

"Were there any witnesses?"

"I'm sure there must have been but I was so embarrassed and confused that I ran until I found a cab and came here."

Ranetti hoped no one from Bel Reame had witnessed the event. This was just the kind of juicy tidbit they loved exchanging over canapes.

Dindino sat up and put his arms around Ranetti. "What should I do?"

"I'm not sure. Even though you're in the right legally, you don't want to bring charges. We'd become *the* topic of gossip for weeks."

87

"Who said anything about bringing charges? All I want is my stuff back, the motorcycle, the watch and the chain. That's all."

"Love will come to your rescue." Ranetti thought, Did I say that? "I'll replace everything for you tomorrow. Please, baby, everything will be all right. Stop crying, it's O.K."

Dindino's face brightened instantly. "You know, I'd kind of outgrown the Honda anyhow."

"You've decided to give up that two-wheeled deathtrap?"

"No. Not at all. I want a BMW, instead. It's so much more chic."

In for a penny, in for a pound. Ranetti, in a fit of generosity, said, "O.K. We'll get you a BMW. For now, come here and give me a hug. Tell me you love me."

"I love you so much," Dindino said, unbuttoning the top of his jeans.

The Empress smiled. How easy it is to make him happy, he thought.

The next morning, the Empress was having second thoughts. In the course of one hour he had written three checks, one for the BMW, one for the Rolex and one to his jeweler for the gold chain. Ranetti was in a down mood.

Dindino, on the other hand, was the picture of happiness. He was cruising up and down the streets of Milan, the catbird seat under him, perched on a spanking new, fully equipped BMW.

With the thought that Dindino was taken care of, it was now time to get down to business. Ranetti started going through the mail. A yellow envelope, marked *Priority*, with no return address caught his eye. With a slight feeling of trepidation, he reached for it and opened it. Inside was a single typewritten page.

Dear Asshole,
    Your blond boyfriend fucks you in bed. Outside of bed he screws you. Take a trip to Sicily, especially Palermo. Many women will be wearing Ranetti furs. None of which were

bought from you. Your sweet Dindino steals them, sends them south, where certain friends of your boyfriend knock off your designs and eat into your profits. Are you not pleased to know your protege has the true entrepreneurial talent?

Dindino is so self-assured in his little sideline, he no longer bothers to be cautious. You should have no trouble discovering the truth of the matter.

One other thing. Dindino brags that it is he who wears the pants in the family. In certain circles, this tends to make you a laughing stock.

As usual, you're the last to find out. How fortunate you are to have a friend to open your eyes.

A Friend

Ranetti was flabbergasted. He couldn't believe what he'd just read. Could it be true? That is, could the part about the fur rip-off be true? As he knew, and he thought no one else did, the part about who wears the pants in the family was resoundingly true.

He was lavish in his treatment of Dindino—he showered him with gifts—the BMW was certain proof of that. He took him to the finest, most expensive restaurants and clubs. It must be the small monthly "allowance" check. Aside from Dindino's slight paycheck at the workshop, that was his only real source of income and it was—face the truth—minuscule.

Ranetti was at sixes and sevens. He couldn't live in this kind of suspicion, this kind of doubt. He'd have to hire a private detective.

A bundle of nerves, not knowing what to do, he reached into a desk drawer for an upper, which he then washed down with a slug of Johnny Walker Black.

He was nerving himself for the outdoors. He hated going out. It was filled with weather—that was for poor people. It was also filled with insects of all kinds.

Stepping out into the overwhelming mugginess of a typical Milan summer's day, he cursed Dindino under his breath.

He sensed Dindino was not innocent. Some inner alarm bell, some premonitory feeling was edging him toward a state of agitation.

He couldn't find a cab anywhere. After five minutes of futile searching, the upper went off inside him like a cherry bomb.

Across the street he noticed Laura Maramani. She was a celebrated fashion writer—celebrated most, in fact, for her one line assessments etched in acid.

Although Ranetti took a rather benign attitude toward critics, he was still smarting from an article she'd written about his collection a month before. Her irony was as subtle as a sledgehammer, but effective nonetheless. Everyone loved reading her column—except when they themselves were the chosen target.

Maramani was one of the great gossipmongers. If she didn't know something, even if it hadn't happened yet, it wasn't worth knowing. Maybe she had written that poisonous note. The heat, the frustration, the upper were all converging on Ranetti.

He looked over at her. She caught his eye and waved, grinning. Ranetti flipped out. Waving back he yelled, "Fuck you, baby." She looked at him puzzled. He held up the middle finger of his left hand. "Come on, baby. Hop, I'll catch you."

Just then a cab appeared from nowhere. Ranetti leaped into it, told the driver, "Corso Sempione," and collapsed against the back of the seat. Laura Maramani shrugged and walked on. An everyday occurrence in her line of work.

If it turned out Dindino was guilty of the accusations in that letter, Ranetti thought in the cab, he'll pay for this. He will *pay* for this.

The investigator took ten days to dig up all the evidence. Dindino *was* a thief, and there was a lively underground dealing in Ranetti furs in Sicily.

Ranetti wrote out the exorbitant check without batting an eyelash. He asked the investigator for something to drink.

"Will that be all, sir?"

"Yes, the drink is fine."

"I wasn't referring to the drink."

"Oh, how dense of me. Well, I would like to teach Dindino a lesson and I'm certainly not going to go through legal channels."

"You're not going to press charges in court then, sir?"

"No. I think private chastisement would be more effective."

"May I congratulate you, sir. You've come to the right place, again."

"Have you any suggestions?" Ranetti was smiling for the first time in ten days. It was a vindictive smile.

Dindino didn't have to be overly sensitive to realize that for the last ten days, since the BMW in fact, something was wrong. The Empress had turned cold, frigid in fact. The stream of poetry had frozen.

Dindino wasn't too worried. He assumed it was a passing mood, maybe some business problem. Dindino was having no such problems. He had saved up a tidy sum already and the black-market fur business would soon double its turnover.

He came out of Burghy's to see three punks standing around the BMW gawking. That's how it is when you drive a BMW.

He arrived at the BMW and greeted the guys, wanting to seem just one of the boys himself. He was so proud of his machine.

All three jumped him at once, punching, kicking, holding him down.

"No!" he shouted. "Don't you hurt me. I'll give you whatever you want. Take my wallet."

A cleverly placed chop behind the ear put him out and ended all discussion. He awoke on the floor of a jalopy, moving pretty fast too. He was totally trussed up, like a Christmas turkey. There were only two of the original three men in the car.

"Listen, guys. You can have the BMW too."

"You can't give us what we already have," one of them said.

A chill ran up Dindino's spine. He realized this wasn't some ordinary robbery. He was in some kind of serious trouble.

"Listen," he pleaded, "if you let me go, I . . . "

Another punch put him under. He had no idea how long the journey was. Every time he surfaced they put him under again. Who could be behind this? Teo? Ranetti?

Finally the long drive was over. They dragged him out of the car. His legs were so cramped he couldn't stand up by himself. He looked around—deserted countryside. Then he realized how familiar it looked—it was his native Sicily.

Before he could say anything, one of the others said, "You're lucky pal. It could have been a lot worse. You're lucky you're not getting iced. Our client just wants to teach you a little lesson. He says he never wants to see your face anywhere in Milan again."

It hit home, then. Ranetti must have found out about the fur sideline.

From somewhere in the car, two lead pipes appeared.

Stumbling backward, truly horrified now, Dindino shouted "No!"

He made a feeble attempt to run away. They easily caught up with him. One on each side, in no time, they had broken both his knees. Dindino had been taught a lesson.

Chapter 9

" "A hundred miles of virgin shoreline. You will feel as if you've been transported to a different continent, a different era—perhaps the stone age."

"Signor Vinci, for a real-estate man you certainly can get poetic." Diana Rau smiled. She glanced at her watch. Her fiancé, Kao Misokubi, should have been here by now.

"These parts are so virgin, so primitive, it's easy to get lost here." He too was waiting for Kao's appearance.

From the promontory, the rugged Sardinian coast was devoid of any man-made feature, not a house, not a telephone line. Way off in the distance there were a few power lines, but they were so few, so far off they themselves seemed a mirage.

This will all be mine, Diana thought, at least on paper. Kao was buying it in her name because, according to Italian law, being a foreigner, he couldn't own more than two acres. (The Aga

Khan had cleverly gotten around that simple law by forming a consortium, but Kao did not want to be responsible to a contentious board of strangers.)

"Here they come!"

A car appeared, chugging up the semi-private road. Out of it got two men, associates of Signor Vinci. One of them said, "We've just received word from Mr. Misokubi. He's been held up in Rome by a sudden airline strike."

"We'll go ahead anyhow," Diana said.

One of Vinci's men began to blather on about how the area would benefit from an influx of tourists. Even Nature itself would benefit.

Diana tuned him out. In her own mind she was envisioning bulldozers cutting a coast road into the landscape, cottage, villas, golf courses, malls, yacht clubs. The Arab Coast would be the most chichi vacation spot yet. Maybe even a race course. She'd leave that kind of decision to the architects. She might even contemplate the notion of a handful of poor people—someone would have to cut hair, serve drinks, mow lawns. That way, with workers' housing built way off somewhere out of sight, they could qualify for a lot of government subsidies.

Diana came back to the conversation to hear Vinci say, "Of course, there still is the snake problem."

"Did you say snakes?"

"Very big ones, the area's full of them."

A bit uneasy, Diana instinctively looked to the ground.

"Of course a large settlement of humans will aggravate the ecology," Vinci went on. "That's because the humans will drive out the snakes' natural enemies."

Reaching out her hand, Diana said, "Meet one of the snakes' natural enemies. Seriously, are they poisonous?"

"No, but they'll certainly frighten the tourists."

"What do they eat?"

"Lizards and voles, mostly."

"What do the lizards and voles eat?"

94

"Various kinds of insects."

"We'll hire a crop duster and spray and spray and spray. First we'll get rid of the insects, finally the snakes. We might have to use some DDT." Diana looked at Vinci.

"DDT is technically illegal," he said, but with a wink he added, "Of course if we officially never find out . . . "

"Is there anything else you'd like to see, Ms. Rau?"

"Yes. I want to see the coastline from the sea. My friends are waiting for me in a boat at Santa Teresa di Gallura."

The boat, a 100-foot Benetti of Panamanian registry, sailed very slowly along the Arab Coast. The guests were luxuriating in the scenery.

"It's an earthly paradise," said the Senator. He was dressed in tan- colored shorts and loud shirt. Though an Italian, his clothes made him look like a German tourist. He and his guests were eating some homemade gelato, or more precisely, yacht-made gelato. The Senator had a passion for ice cream. It was a small party. Kao being absent, that left Diana, the Senator, the Senator's secretary and two young and vacuous female models. Although from all reports all he did was look, the Senator liked surrounding himself with beautiful women.

"There it is," he said to Diana.

"All I see is rock."

"It's impossible at this distance to distinguish between the granite of the reef, the vegetation and the villa itself." The architect had built the villa almost as if it were cascading down the side of the slope, having been inspired by the principals of Frank Lloyd Wright—that houses should blend with their environment. He was eminently successful at this.

"Kind of a luxury pueblo," Diana quipped.

The Senator handed her some binoculars.

Holding them to her eyes, she asked if there were other guests.

"No, just the domestic personnel."

"There's a boy on the beach who looks like he'd be very handy around the house," she said as she handed back the binoculars.

The Senator scanned the beach until he got the lad into focus. He lay absolutely still on his back, his mammoth erection pointing toward the general direction of Rome.

"That's my chauffeur."

"He seems the excitable type."

"Who knows? The heat of the sun. A delicious dream," the Senator said casually.

Something was stirring inside Diana she didn't want to name. Lamely she added, "He has a wonderful body."

"Do you think so?" the Senator inquired ever so casually.

It was after the noonday meal. The maid was serving—surprise—ice cream on one of the upper terraces. Diana took the opportunity to slip away. She took the beautifully sculpted staircases down, down the side of the boulder until she reached the beach. From here she couldn't be seen from the upper terraces.

The young chauffeur was still asleep in the sun. His erection had abated, but soft it was still phenomenal. Its tip rested neatly on top of his belly button. Diana thought, If that were a snake, now, I'd be terrified.

Instead she was fascinated. That strange feeling was welling up inside her again. She took off all her clothes and draped them on a nearby set of bushes. It had been a long time since she'd felt this kind of excitement. Maybe it was the sheer size of the thing. Now that she thought about it, had she ever seen anything that large before—on a human at least? She tiptoed over to the sleeping figure. Her hand was drawn to the object as if by magnetic attraction. It was perfectly soft and still larger than any man's she'd ever experienced. She touched it. The lad arose with a start. Then, reassured by her smile, he leaned back on his elbows and waited to see what she would do.

She straddled his middle and was manipulating his cock back to hardon status. By the time it got there Diana was equally ready. She managed—somehow she managed—to get the whole thing inside of her and to ease herself down on him until the pressure made her gasp and catch her breath.

"What's your name?" she whispered.

"Andrea."

"I'm Diana Rau. I want to fuck you." She took a very deep breath and let him slide the rest of the way into her.

"You lie still. I'll take care of this." She'd never been so master-ly, so take-charge. That in itself was a turnon.

"How much does the Senator pay you."

"Five thousand liras a month."

"Come back to Milan with me. I need a chauffeur. I'll tri-ple what he pays you."

"Would we fuck like this in Milan too, Diana?"

Suddenly furious, yet without stopping the up and down rhythm, she said, "Don't call me by my first name, ever. Especially when we're fucking."

From the deepest part inside her there arose a rumble that grew into a full-blown explosion. Diana came with a shriek. A few seconds later, she could feel Andrea coming inside her. There was so much it felt like a douche. They lay there panting for a bit.

She finally extricated herself from him, gave him her Milan address, and leaned over and kissed him on the cheek.

"What else do you do for the Senator besides driving his car?" she asked unable to hold back the jealous tone.

"Nothing. I swear. Sometimes he comes to my bedroom, but all he does is look and then goes away."

Chapter 10

*T*he very idea of dealing with Ugo Varanni made Ciaccio a little queasy in the stomach. If a task called for a ratcatcher, one called a ratcatcher and didn't get overly sensitive on the subject. Besides, Alvise, the perfect avatar, would actually be dealing with Varanni, not the Big Turk himself.

Now that Rick's return was in the works, Ciaccio would have thought that his future happiness would dominate his thoughts. He knew he had a feeling of vindictiveness, but he had no idea it was so strong. All night long he had been tossing and turning in bed, unable to sleep, his thoughts dominated by this *idée fixe:* revenge on Diovisi. He was sure—sure as God made young boys, that Diovisi had caused his beloved Rick to flee in the first place. He must get even, extremely even. Forgive and forget was not one of his favorite mottos.

Periodically he would flash on future scenes of happiness with

Rick, but these daydreams only helped fuel his desire to see Diovisi get his.

He rejected the idea of torching Diovisi's workrooms—after all the brouhaha, Diovisi would be the object of everyone's compassion and Ciaccio couldn't stand the prospect of that.

The biggest hurdle—Sabina's compliance in the arranged marriage—had been jumped. It was easier than one might have guessed. Once Venanzi was out of the way (what a pushover that had been), it was merely a matter of firm negotiation. Sabina said she would come up with a list of things—Ciaccio, taking a deep breath, knew it would be spectacular, but that he would comply and all would be smooth sailing from then on.

It must have been the idea of revenge that kept Ciaccio going—he had been working steadily all day and all night on the new collection, but he found he was only tired, not sleepy.

Getting up, he went to his escritoire to get an upper—a fifteen milligram spansule of dexadrine. If he was going to stay up and have his mind race feverishly, then he'd do it in style. He took two, washing them down with a slug of Chivas *réserve spéciale*. Then he sat down and waited for the hit.

The wait was not a long one—he hadn't eaten for several hours. Wham! Ten minutes later it hit him full force, like a mule kick to the head. Ten thousand volts burst through his body. He felt the need to do something physical—chop wood, shovel snow, climb the Santa Scala on his knees.

His brain was whirling so violently that for a moment all cerebral activity canceled itself out and he stood stupefied, not even knowing where he was. Then he remembered. Vendetta! Diovisi ground into the mud!

From Ciaccio's point of view, they were not even direct competitors. Irone Fashions appealed to the very well-heeled, the international set. Diovisi, to his mind at least, catered more to the bourgeois taste, the upper middle classes who liked their sheets, shirts and, if possible, socks signed by a designer. Diovisi was even known now and then to cater to the masses—giving interviews in the Sunday supplements of the popular newspapers.

If Ciaccio had any competitor, he preferred to think it was Valentino. Of course this wasn't anywhere near true, but Ciaccio fed his fantasies off the image. Valentino was a decent, honorable man, splendidly isolated with his fifty or so clients, the richest women in the world. He was a gentleman of the old school, like Dior or Balenciaga.

Diovisi, on the other hand, could not have offered a greater contrast. His peasant face, thick with artfully applied makeup, repelled Ciaccio. Since Ciaccio came from southern-Italian peasant stock too, perhaps it was a matter of like repelling like. He also hated Zaco Ottoboni, who had also clawed his way up to the top from a peasant background. Ottoboni, called the Moor of Venice, had made his name in knitwear of impossible color combinations.

He could go on like this forever. He must put his thoughts in order. That speed was something else. His brain was racing but it couldn't sort out the important from the trivial.

In an effort to control himself, Ciaccio grabbed a piece of paper and started hunting for some writing instrument. Not being able right away to get his hands on a pencil, pen or Magic Marker, he grabbed a lipstick. He sat down with the blank sheet of paper on a board across his lap.

UGO VARANNI. IT TAKES A PRICK TO CATCH A PRICK. He wrote the sentence twice and underlined it. He pressed so hard, the lipstick broke. He angrily hurled the lipstick against the wall where it left a vermilion smudge. He must call Alvise. Now, this instant.

Alvise answered on the fourth ring. His "hello" was so swallowed it sounded as if he were speaking through a pillow.

"What took you so long to answer the phone?"

"I was asleep. Do you know what time it is?"

"I'll play your silly game. What time is it?"

"It's seven-thirty A.M. You kept us all up till after three last night. If you don't mind—"

"Whatever it is, I mind. Get your ass over here. Pronto."

In a state less than pulled together, Alvise arrived within ten minutes. Waiting is the hardest thing of all to do on speed so Ciaccio decided to shower. Yes, a Scottish shower—alternately hot, then cold. Having worked out his plan of revenge, at least in broad outline, against Diovisi, he could now afford to concentrate his thoughts on Rick. Before stepping into the stream of the shower he went to his night table to get the photo of his beloved Rick that sat there. Naked, by the side of a pool, he looked like he could have been sculpted by Phidias. Ciaccio took the photo and returning to the bathroom, propped it up next to the tub.

Stripping, he discovered himself with a raging hardon. Though it was quite possible this was one of the effects of the speed, Ciaccio preferred to think it was caused by his romantic thoughts of Rick. He looked at the photo—that stunning smile, those dewy and fathomless eyes . . .

Ignoring the torrents of pouring water, Ciaccio began to jerk off. His penis took on a life of its own. He couldn't remember the last time it had been so hard, so responsive to touch. His orgasm roared over him.

"Oh, Rick, baby, Rick . . . "

He shot a huge load, almost all of it hitting the photo of Rick, covering his face. Wiped out, Ciaccio collapsed in a heap on the floor. The shower kept running.

That was how Alvise found him. Alvise was the only person who had a key to the apartment besides Rick, that is.

He stood at the doorway to the bathroom and took in the scene. The pouring water, Ciaccio collapsed in front of Rick's photo, the photo dripping jism—there was no mistaking that. All perfectly understandable. Compared to some of the things Alvise had witnessed over the years, positively romantic.

Time to wake up the resident genius, thought Alvise as he stooped over. He grasped Ciaccio gingerly by the shoulder.

"Here I am," he said, when he saw Ciaccio cock open an eye.

"What do you want?"

"I should ask you that. Whether you remember or not, you

102

called me and told me to come right on over."

It was amazing. Maybe the speed was still working. One minute Ciaccio was a total wreck, the next a man totally in charge. He got up, slipped into his raw-silk robe, ran his hands through his hair and strode into the other room, every inch the head of a multi-million-dollar firm.

"You're right," he said. "I did call you. I have something important to tell you. It's about Diovisi." He was looking for the sheet of paper he had scrawled on in lipstick.

"If you want the latest news, Diovisi is working round the clock. The advance word is his collection is going to blow the whole industry wide open." Alvise knew this was just the thing to say to whet Ciaccio's competitive instinct.

"Not the way mine will! Let's see if we can't have his collection blow up in his face instead."

"Do I detect a note of pique in your voice?"

"He shouldn't have fucked around with Rick and me."

"From his point of view, you started it all, two years ago when you stole that goon he used as a bodyguard from him."

"How can you compare the two? I stole a goon. He wrecked my life. Or tried to."

"Some people might think Rick gave in a bit too quickly."

"Whose side are you on, mine or Diovisi's?"

"Yours, of course. But I don't think you should escalate this to a civil war. The matter's settled. Rick's coming back. Sabina will marry him and you'll all live happily ever after. Let it go. The past is past."

"Not on your ass! That bastard has got to be made to understand that by fucking with Ciaccio Irone's love life he went too far. He breaks my balls, I'll break his. If he's got any, which I doubt."

"If you want to stop his show, there are a slew of things you can do—fill the auditorium with mice, for instance."

"Be serious, Alvise. A prank like that would only get him more publicity—free publicity no less. I don't think your mind's working too well this morning."

"Why should it? It's crying out for sleep."

"Well mine's working swell. I've got a great plan."

Alvise never failed to be amazed at Ciaccio's resourcefulness, his resiliency. It only confirmed in his mind that the right people after all achieved fame and fortune. In business, it always helped to be one part cobra.

"Don't you want to know my plan?"

"Don't tease me. Of course I'm dying to find out."

"First, get Ugo Varanni."

"Ick, is that really necessary?"

"I'm afraid so. Tell him to infiltrate Diovisi's workshop. *He'll* know of a way. I want photos of all his collection."

"Ugo Varanni!"

"Get over it, Alvise. One has to use the appropriate tool for a job. Offer him whatever sum it'll take, no matter how much. Promise him from now on we'll even use the whores from his agency. But be sure he does what we want."

"In my name, of course."

"Of course. If anything goes wrong, I have to be above it all. Like Richard Nixon."

Alvise thought this an unfortunate analogy, but remained silent.

"Do this job right, and when the whole affair blows over, I'll get you that boutique in Cinisello you seem to lust after."

"Cinisello!"

"Cinisello, wherever you like. You know better than I which provincial boutiques have the highest turnovers."

"I'll gladly settle for Cinisello."

All I have do to is approach Varanni, Alvise thought. Somewhere in the pit of his stomach something rebelled, but he ignored the feeling.

Chapter 11

$\mathcal{U}$p shit creek without a paddle. Again. So what else was new? Ugo Varanni was returning from the casino of Campione without a lira to his name. His last loose change for the highway tolls he had scraped up from the back of the glove compartment. He was back in Milan but he had no desire to go home to Giovanna, and her cowlike understanding eyes. If only she weren't so compliant, so understanding.

Once again he found himself returning penniless to face the mountain of unpaid bills and hounding creditors. Cleaned out at blackjack and roulette. Would his luck never turn?

He was also down to the last few drops of gas—the indicator had been in the red area indicating empty for the last several miles. He pulled over and parked—or maybe the car just stopped, it was hard to tell—near the seaplane base to look at the water. It wasn't as if he were contemplating suicide. He wouldn't have to. The way his luck was running there were any number of his creditors who would gladly help him over the threshold into the next world.

The water was sludgy, filled with oil and various kinds of floating debris. It was a measure of Varanni's state of mind that this view, and its concomitant smells, could ease his mind. It calmed him down somehow. He sat there for hours, maybe he even dozed off for a bit.

His head was abuzz with the sound of little clicking balls falling into slots, croupiers calling out "Place your bets. Place your bets."

It was around ten in the morning. He decided to go home and face the music. He knew all too well what lay in store for him and it wasn't all that musical. Another day of anguish and anxiety. Avoiding creditors and making excuses to others. At least they couldn't reach him by phone—he wasn't able to pay last month's bill and had had the service discontinued.

Giovanna was there, greeting him, oozing warmth and understanding. She had some coffee warming on the back of the stove.

"How did things go?"

"How the fuck do you think things went?" he exploded at her.

She poured him some coffee and sat down at the kitchen table with him.

He sipped the coffee and wrinkled his face in a look of disgust. "Why can't you even make a decent cup of coffee?"

Giovanna sat there stolidly, a little smile at the corner of her lips. Her capacity for abuse seemed limitless. It all rolled off her back. Giovanna was a remarkably attractive woman, if tending a bit toward the full-figured.

Varanni thought she was too calm, too submissive. He unconsciously blamed her for all his failures. Maybe if she were more aggressive, more combative.

"I made the coffee in our old espresso machine," she said. "I think it needs to be replaced. If we could see our way toward getting a new one . . . "

Varanni put down his half-filled cup and viciously turned on her.

"We owe money to half of Milan. We're soon going to be evicted. The telephone's already been discontinued. How can you think about an espresso machine!?"

"The telephone's working, *caro*."

"How did you pull off that little miracle?"

"I paid the bill yesterday."

"Without consulting me first of course."

"If I'd have told you, you'd've taken the money to gamble with as well. And then Mittaglia couldn't have called."

Ugo suddenly sat up. He was all ears. "Who called?"

"Alvise Mittaglia."

"What did he want?"

"He didn't say. He left a number. He wants you to call as soon as you can."

Varanni dashed for the other room, where the phone was. En route he stopped to fondle Giovanna's breasts in thanks. He felt her nipples harden immediately.

"You know, you still have great boobs, Giovanna."

"Thank you, Ugo. They're yours anytime. I just wish you'd take more advantage of them."

"It's because I'm always so worried. My cock can't seem to stand at attention when there are always creditors at the door. You sure feel awfully good right now."

Giovanna clutched his wrists at her breasts. "I'm always ready, Ugo."

"I must call Mittaglia right away. You get into bed and spread your thighs. I'll be there in two shakes."

Varanni had Mittaglia's number on his Rolodex. The number he had left with Giovanna was a different one.

Curious, Varanni dialed hastily. He wondered what Mittaglia could want. He was one of the eighteen people in all of Milan Varanni didn't owe any money to. Maybe he had bought one of Varanni's IOUs. No, not possible. Mittaglia never came into contact with the world that was populated by Varanni's creditors.

It couldn't be about a model either. Mittaglia meant Irone Fashions which meant real class. Varanni was strictly bargain basement, closer to the bordello than Bel Reame.

The phone was ringing. No answer. Please, Varanni begged, let someone be there. He was about to have a heart attack. If only he hadn't stopped at the seaplane base and stared at all that oil and floating condoms for hours.

"Hello." It was Mittaglia, thank God.

"This is Ugo Varanni. My secretary tells me you called."

"Yes. I need you for something."

"Just tell me how I can be of use to you, Signor Mittaglia."

"Not on the phone. When can we meet?"

"Right away if you like."

"Fine. Meet me in one hour outside the Astor Cinema. I'll be waiting in a gray Saab Turbo."

"One hour. I'll be there. Count on me."

Varanni hung up and mused, Mittaglia has a job for me but it can't be one that's too kosher. Otherwise he wouldn't be playing these spy games of secrecy. A meeting where no one would notice them.

Crossing his fingers, he hoped it would be something big and important, something that might put a nice bit of change into his pocket. The fact that Mittaglia had called personally seemed promising—it was something he didn't trust a secretary to handle.

Varanni remembered Giovanna, lying in the bed. Now he was too excited by the prospect of the meeting with Mittaglia. He really wasn't in the mood for fucking. But she was lying in the bedroom and he'd have to go in to get the subway fare.

There she was, sprawled out naked, her thighs wide apart. Obedient and submissive as ever. She was playing with herself and Varanni began to respond.

He had been fucking her since she was sixteen. She had some magic power over him. Now, many years later, the very sight of her naked was enough to stir him to a frenzy.

108

"Well, *caro*. How'd it go?" Her speech was slurred. She had turned herself on.

Varanni swallowed, trying to ignore the urgent feeling in his crotch. "I'm in a hurry. I have to meet Mittaglia in less than an hour. And I have to go by subway. The tank's empty."

"That'll give us more than enough time. You always say how much you like quickies."

Varanni gave up the struggle. He tore off his clothes and in no time he was on top of her, viciously pumping away. She was moaning, clutching him with her legs.

He came in almost no time at all. As soon as he did he stopped pumping. Another moment and he was standing up getting dressed again. She lay on the bed moaning, turning from side to side, using her hand to get herself off.

She looked up at him with her soulful, trusting eyes. Whatever he had done for her, she had made him feel serene, relaxed. The quickie had just hit the spot, relieving his tension. He felt on top of the world. He *knew* Mittaglia was sure to offer him something big and important.

There's a moral here, he thought. Don't ever give up, no matter how dark it seems.

"Was it good for you, *caro*?" Giovanna asked. He hadn't noticed if she had come.

"It was great, baby. You're the best. You're the only one who can get me to rise to the occasion."

"It's a shame it happens so rarely," she murmured.

"Everything's going to be different, baby. You'll see. We'll go on a fabulous cruise around the world. The South Seas, Polynesia, the Indian Ocean . . . "

"Let's do it again."

"I can't. There's no time. This appointment is crucial. I have to shave and get to the train station."

"No, you don't. There's still 20,000 liras left in my bag. You can use if for gas."

"Where'd it come from?"

"I was saving up for a present for you."

"I'll use it for a cab. I don't want to be late."

Mittaglia was already waiting in the Saab when Varanni arrived at the Astor Cinema.

He opened the passenger door and slid into the seat. Without saying hello, he asked for a cigarette.

Alvise offered him one, lighting it with a gold Cartier lighter.

"Nice lighter," Varanni said. "I used to have one just like it but I lost it somewhere."

"If you do this job for me and do it well you'll easily be able to buy yourself another one. Maybe even a set of wheels like this," he said, patting the Saab's steering wheel.

Varanni whistled, impressed. "Who do I have to kill?" He was only half joking. Both of them knew it.

"Nobody. You just have to break a few balls on a ballbreaker."

"Would I be risking jail?"

"Not if you play your cards right. And don't blab your head off to anyone."

"I'll be as silent as a mime. Tell me the name of this ballbreaker."

"Lorenzo the Magnificent."

Varanni let out another whistle, not unlike the first one. This was big game. And the hunting preserve was Bel Reame.

"Lorenzo Diovisi?" Varanni had to make absolutely sure they were talking the same language. This was no time for nicknames.

"The same. Like all of us in Bel Reame, he's preparing his next collection. Of course he works under wraps. It's up to you to get under those wraps."

"I could get him to hire one of my models."

"Dream on. I don't want to offend you but your merchandise is strictly remnant sale. Your models have fingerprints all over them. Or needle tracks."

"But that's not true anymore, Signor Mittaglia."

"Bullshit, Varanni. We can't afford the slightest hitch in this

110

operation."

"I'll need time."

"One week. That's the time frame. By the end of the week Lorenzo's entire collection has to be photographed and the pictures have to be in my hands."

"How much for me?"

"Fifty million liras, plus expenses, of course," Alvise said, knowing he'd charge Ciaccio triple and keep the difference for himself.

"That's a fair price. But I want the expense money up front. You know, to move freely . . . "

"I've thought of that."

Alvise pulled out a thick envelope from the glove compartment, and handed it to the desperate man.

"There's five million liras here. If you split with that money, don't bother ever showing your face in Milan again."

"What do you take me for?"

"For precisely what you are—scum. My advice is, Get your shit together. With the money you'll make from this deal, you could pay many of your debts, become solvent again."

"Don't worry, Signor Mittagglia. I promise you those photos—even if I have to get dressed in drag and get them myself."

"I admire your zeal, but I think you should find some less dramatic method. I'll call you every morning at eleven."

It's amazing how different the world looks when there's a lot of money in one's pockets—especially pockets long used to being empty.

Tonight—after purchasing a few new silk shirts and the like—he'd try the casinos at Campione again. Of course, he'd get the job done too. It would be easy enough to find out which models were working for Diovisi.

He might need Giovanna's help on that. She had an encyclopedic memory for the names and faces of models. Feeling more tender toward Giovanna, he stepped into a store and bought her a new espresso machine. She'd be in seventh heaven over it.

Life could be the shits, but now and then it could be a beautiful thing too. Especially if one had money. And the prospect of a big chance. Varanni knew this was only the beginning. Once he'd gotten the photos for Mittaglia, it would only be the start of a long-term and fruitful partnership. He'd make himself indispensable. He'd start a really first-class modeling agency. The sky was the limit.

Chapter 12

Kao Misokubi was not the greatest lover in the world—at least as far as his technique was concerned. He acted the way he did in the business world—every move was calculated in advance, one move led to another and he was already five moves ahead in his calculations. That's what made him seem so cool in bed—he was so calculating. Passion, feeling, never had a chance to emerge and throw off the game plan.

Diana had kept him dangling for as long as she dared. Since he traveled so much, that wasn't too hard. She had held off giving herself (or at least her body) to him until he had gotten the Arab Coast for her. A token, so to speak, that he trusted her. And Diana needed him to trust her if she were to launch her own fashion empire, with him as chief backer.

Whatever else Kao was, he was a gifted businessman and he was no one's fool. Even if no amount of money was involved. Diana

113

had held off discussing Diana Rau Fashions, until one night, after a bout of sex, Kao brought it up himself.

Though he didn't sound it, he certainly looked cynical as he asked her, "How much is this going to cost me, darling?"

Diana, pretending to misunderstand, said, "If you think you can buy me off the way you usually buy your thousand-dollar lays, think again."

"What do you know about my, uh, other bed partners?"

"I confess, I did a little investigating. While you were investigating me, in fact."

"We could have used the same agency and saved some bucks."

Kao smiled at his own little joke. "I discovered, for instance, that you dropped your Pier, whatever-his-last-name-was, the second you knew I was returning to Italy."

Diana said, "It seemed the only proper thing to do under the circumstances. Besides, he was beginning to get on my nerves."

"Still, I'm grateful he's gone. I'd like to think you dumped him for me."

"That's not *so* far from the truth."

"According to my informants, there's nobody else in your life except me anyhow."

Diana immediately thought of Andrea, the Sardinian hunk she'd stolen from the Senator. So far, at least, her secret was safe. She had better redouble all precautions. Andrea was beginning to become a habit and she didn't want to give him up under any circumstances. It was the first time in her life a passion had emerged and she had too little experience in dealing with the real thing.

Kao's question had put her on the alert. Trying to probe deeper, she said, "No kidding, if you think you have to pay me . . ."

Kao said, "Now Diana, you're many things but you're not vulgar. I know you won't hand me a bill. Besides, while I was having you investigated, I had your finances looked into as well. I learned exactly how clever you are with your money."

Diana said, "I'll take that as a compliment. Thank you."

114

Kao continued, "Also it's apparent that a woman of your stature doesn't take on a Kao Misokubi just because her emotions ran away with her. In fact, Diana, I'd be quite disappointed if it turned out your interest in me had no ulterior motive behind it."

Diana said, "This certainly sounds like it's time to put all one's cards on the table. If you know all about my financial situation, then you know I don't need anything or anyone."

"In a manner of speaking," Kao said. "You're so well off you can easily live off your investments for the rest of your life without a moment's worry. But we also can assume, I think, that you have some ambitions, ambitions so grand that you probably could use a good deal of solid help. Am I totally mistaken?"

Kao was smiling enigmatically. He had grasped everything. It was better this way. It would save a lot of time.

Diana took a deep breath and plunged in. "I want to start my own business. After working in the fashion world for so many years, I'm overdue. I want to start my own house. I want it so bad I can taste it. I want to compete with Irone and Diovisi and show them I can beat them at their own game."

"I'm sure you can," Kao said, getting serious.

"*You* know it and *I* know it. But I want the world to know. I want my own store on Fifth Avenue. I want the cover of *Time* and *Newsweek* and *People*."

"And you're counting on my money to back you in all this?"

Diana looked him in the eye. "I'm counting on you, period. I'm counting on your intelligence, your experience, your advice."

"Diana, don't gush. That'll be enough of that." Kao burst out laughing. Had he seen through her all along? Was he just teasing her, like a cat with a half-dead mouse?

Diana's face fell. "Kao, maybe I'm mistaken but I thought, you and I . . . "

"Don't worry, Diana. If you hadn't brought the whole thing up I would have in the next couple of days. I would have advised you to start your own line. With my backing, of course. If you've been going to bed with me just to make me agreeable to that idea, you've been wasting your ammunition—I know a good investment when I see one, after all."

Diana smiled with relief. "I would have gone to bed with you anyway, Kao, *caro*. I really like you." That's not a lie, she thought to herself—she didn't say love, just like. She hugged him.

"You couldn't make a wiser investment if you tried. Do you have any special conditions?"

"We'll be partners. Fifty-fifty."

Diana sat up. "Now, Kao, there's no way that's going to be. Diana Rau Fashions is me—a majority of me, at the very least."

Kao expected this. He admired her for it. "Then what's in it for me?"

Diana said, "Make me an offer. A *reasonable* offer."

"Keep in mind we're talking business, *cara*."

"I am. What do you want for bankrolling me—short of half of everything?"

"I want the exclusive distribution rights for all your models throughout Latin America and the Far East. That's non-negotiable."

"That's more like it. O.K. they're yours. Now let's celebrate."

"Fine. Get out the champagne."

She stroked his genital area. "I was thinking along other lines, actually."

Kao looked at his watch. It was indicative of the man that he never took it off in bed. "Sorry. We'll have to celebrate some other time. I think your idea's great but I have an appointment at the consulate and there's just no time."

Diana heaved another sigh of relief. She thanked the consulate in her head and put her need to celebrate on hold until Kao left when she would go upstairs to the garret room Andrea was occupying.

As soon as Kao left, Diana jumped into the shower and cleaned herself so thoroughly it constituted a form of foreplay. After the shower, she slipped into a satin robe (a gift from Kao) and went upstairs.

116

Andrea was dozing on the bed, as usual naked as a jaybird. His penis was soft, lolling against his stomach. Even totally soft it inspired awe. Diana went over and kissed it affectionately on the tip.

Andrea woke up, half-opening his eyes. He reached over and stroked one of her breasts.

"Did you shower?" he asked.

"What's it to you whether I showered or not?" Diana misunderstood his question entirely. She thought he had asked out of concern for hygiene.

"Don't blow your stack. I thought I smelled that wonderful plum-scented soap you used for showering, that's all." He was starting to get hard. She felt like such a fool for her misunderstanding. The nipple he was holding was hardening along with his cock.

Andrea looked into her eyes. He held her gaze for a long time. Finally he said, "It never occurred to you I might be falling in love with you?"

This was just the wrong thing for Andrea to say at the moment. Coming as it did right after her encounter with Kao, where she felt in total control of the situation, the lack of control a real love affair with Andrea implied could spell disaster. She felt the pressing desire to flee. To flee this gorgeous young man, with the velvety skin and mammoth cock and the insidious ability to make her tingle all over just thinking about him.

She should have said something to put him in his place, to take control of the situation. Instead she felt awash with waves of desire that left her speechless.

She let the robe slip off her and slide down to the floor. She ran her fingers over his cheeks, his lips.

"Do you want me to kiss you, signora?" he asked, turning over and touching her between the thighs. Diana answered by turning him onto his back and climbing on top of him. She put his immense spear of hard flesh into herself and was amazed to discover how incredibly wet she was.

"Call me Diana, goddammit. Call me Diana." She was now

117

totally encasing him.

"When we fuck or all the time?"

"Always." She screamed. "Always," she was writhing. "Always."

She came and let out a sound not far from a shriek. One of the reasons she had always—until now—felt a sense of control over her life was that she never reached orgasm. There were times she had come close, but she only achieved complete orgasm alone. Andrea was the first person to put her over the edge. She lay there exhausted, trembling.

She lay there caressing his face when a wave of fear came over her. She was scared, for the first time, scared of all the feelings this handsome young man was able to make her feel, seemingly without even making an effort.

"You're going to be my downfall," she whispered into his ear.

"If you like, signora, I can go away. Never to return."

She should have taken him up on his offer. Instead she said, "I told you to call me Diana."

"If you like, Diana, I could return to Sardinia, or go back to the Senator."

"And then?"

An ironic smile appeared on his face.

With a philosophic tone, he said, "I'll find someone else. You'll find someone else. I don't suppose either of us will have much difficulty finding someone new."

She felt like slapping that grin right off his face. If she really were in control of her life, she would take his advice. But he was already under her skin. She could do nothing. She closed her eyes.

He slipped out from under her. She felt his absence so strongly it was as if someone had ripped out a piece of herself. Lying on the bed, she reached over and lit a cigarette.

He had gotten up to dress. She watched him slip into his pants and a cotton shirt. He grabbed a bag from the closet and threw some things into it. He ostentatiously did not pack the gold Rolex or the Dunhill lighter, both gifts from Diana.

"There's a plane I can catch if I hurry."

At first Diana thought he was kidding. By the time he was packed and walking toward the door, she didn't know. She panicked.

"Andrea, come back!"

He turned around. "Why, do you want to go through my bag to make sure I didn't steal anything?"

Diana couldn't take this kind of treatment. Holding her hands out imploringly, she repeated, "Andrea, come here."

He walked over to her, insolence oozing out of his very walk.

"Closer," she said, still on the bed.

He came within reach. Diana quickly and expertly unzipped his pants. His cock flopped out, thick as a normal wrist, but still soft. Diana leaned over and started licking it. It started to harden instantly. She went to work, her eyes shut, beads of sweat breaking out on her forehead.

"Hurry up, Diana, I'm going to miss my plane," he said at one point. It made her feel great—he had called her Diana.

As Diana kept at it, tears began to fall from her eyes. She clutched his hips and held him in place, only causing her to gag now and then. He finally came in a massive crescendo of passion. Diana, without even touching herself, had been so turned on that she came again when he did. Finally she leaned back and looked at him with passion-blurred eyes.

"I'll never let you get on that plane," she managed to get out.

He rezipped his fly. "Is that an order?"

Thinking back on her encounter earlier with Kao, she said, "It's a non-negotiable demand."

"In that case, I suppose I'll get back into bed."

"Here, let me fluff up the pillow for you," she said, a smile of immense contentment on her face.

Later on, during dinner, it occurred to Diana that she was happy, that perhaps in all her life she had never been happier. She and Andrea were dining in her apartment. He acted totally at

119

home. What did she think, he had no manners, that he'd dropped from the trees, never having learned how to use the proper tableware? He was the essence of good manners and charm and proper deportment. She was absolutely entranced.

Somewhere in the middle of dinner, Diana's thoughts had a chance to settle a bit. She remembered something Andrea had said when they were in the midst of lovemaking. She was afraid to bring it up, yet she had to. She steeled herself and mustering the courage, said, "Andrea, back upstairs, you said you were in love with me . . . "

"That's true. At least for what it's worth. The love of a guy like me isn't worth much."

Diana was furious. "Stop that! I only asked if it was true."

"It's true. You're the most beautiful woman I ever met. Also the most intelligent. Quite simply, I love you."

"I don't want to sound coy, but I am old enough to be your mother."

"Oh my God, Diana, surely you're not going to get hung up on the age thing. As if love had anything to do with age."

In a panic, Diana hastily mumbled an "excuse me" and ran off into her study. She was a mass of confusions and insecurities. She was falling in love with Andrea.

She needed to pull herself together, to calm herself down. She rummaged through a drawer until she came upon the envelope under some bills. It was coke. The best money could buy. She'd gotten it from Ciaccio and he always had the best.

She was opening the envelope when she realized Andrea had followed her into the study. He leaped to her side and knocked the envelope out of her hand. The coke scattered everywhere, like a very fine snowfall. Diana was furious.

"You just knocked half a million liras out of my hand."

"That stuff is shit, no matter what it costs. I don't want you taking that crap."

"Are you starting to give me orders?"

"Diana, I'm doing it for your sake. You're my woman now.

120

Therefore I feel a need to protect you. Even from yourself, if necessary."

Her anger vanished immediately. She was all melting tenderness.

"So you really care about me?" she asked, seeming like a little girl.

"I told you, Diana, I love you."

Diana felt tears coming to her eyes. She ran to the bathroom. She was afraid to appear so weak, so vulnerable. She kept splashing cold water on her eyes until the swelling from the tears went down. She was about to reapply her makeup when she looked in the mirror and rethought the issue. She wanted Andrea to see her as she really was, in the full mature ripeness of her beauty, without makeup. She was not in her first youth and the sooner she and Andrea confronted that fact, the better for the both of them.

That evening would be the beginning of the future. There would be no tricks or lies. Well, she did run a comb through her hair, but that wasn't the same thing. She gave herself a parting smile, for luck, in the bathroom mirror and returned to Andrea.

He was standing next to the bookcase, reading. She went over to see what held his attention so. It was volume one of *Remembrance of Things Past*.

When he realized she was standing next to him, he said, "It's in mint condition. You've never read it."

"Who has time to read? Besides, the word is out. Proust is very slow-moving."

"I don't agree. You have to savor him, sip him slowly, like a vintage wine."

Diana was truly astounded. "Do you mean to say you've *read* it?"

If the truth be known, he had actually read the first 50 pages, so he fudged by asking, "What's so odd about that?"

Diana put her hand on his back. "I just realized, I don't know you at all. Aside from the fact that you're sensationally attractive and great in bed, I don't know a thing about your past, your

121

dreams . . . "

"Blame the world we live in," he said as he returned the book to its place on the shelf. "It's a shallow world we live in. All that really counts is money."

"Yet you go along with it," she said. "You lived with the Senator, now with me."

"You think I don't disgust myself?"

"Tell me all about you, Andrea. I want to know who you are, where you come from, how you grew up, everything."

"It couldn't be more banal. My father died young and I had to go to work. I got a job as a lifeguard and then the Senator discovered me. Way back then I had dreams of becoming an architect some day. Oh, the dreams I had!"

All at once, it seized Diana—she knew what she had to do. She'd restore Andrea's dreams, his ambitions.

Beaming with inspiration she said, "You've got to go back to school. I will brook no contradiction. That's an order. You *will* become an architect. It's never too late to realize that kind of dream. And I'll be there at your side all the time."

He looked at her, his eyes glowing with hope. He looks like a child, she thought, a child whose fairy godmother has just made his greatest wish come true.

Now she had two goals in life. She had to launch her own fashion house and she had to help launch Andrea in his own particular dream.

It had been quite a day.

Chapter 13

"Owww!" Ciaccio was shrieking his head off.

The old Chinese man stopped, needle in midair. "If you like, we can end today's session now."

The old man started gathering up the tools of his trade, the needles, the ink pots, the disinfectant.

Not hearing any contradiction from Ciaccio, he said, "I shall take my leave."

"Yeah, go, goodbye," Ciaccio mumbled, wiping tears from his eyes.

It didn't matter to him that the old man was costing him $1000 a day (not counting expenses) everyday he stayed in Milan. He had done the Prince of Savoy's back piece, the talk of three continents. The old man had been flown in from Hong Kong.

"You could have gotten someone from Paris," Alvise had suggested.

Ciaccio had answered, "This is a tattoo. You don't fuck around with something like this. You get the best." And the old man was really number one. He had worked on Lord Mountbatten, the King of Denmark, and the Japanese Emperor.

The old man had just left and Ciaccio was lying on the table moaning steadily. Alvise entered with a bounce in his step to announce, "Rick's in the air. He's flying to your arms right now via TWA."

Ciaccio moaned. "That means he should be here pretty soon."

"Tonight." Alvise looked at Ciaccio's chest. He tried to hide his real feelings, a combination of horror, disgust and amazement, when he said, "It's coming along. The old man's doing a good job. Is it very painful, I wonder?"

Ciaccio, leaping up, cast Alvise a look that could kill for his last remark and said, "Call him back. Catch him before he leaves."

"The old man? I just bumped into him at the elevator."

"Run after him. Catch him. The tattoo must be finished by tonight when Rick arrives."

A few minutes later, Alvise reentered with the old Chinese tattooist.

Ciaccio spread himself out on his table of pain once again. At least his suffering would be finite. It would all be over by this evening. Soon he'd be holding Rick in his arms again.

"Did you change your mind?"

"Yes," Ciaccio said. "It must be all done by this evening."

Was there the hint of a smile on the old man's face as he said, "It will be very painful."

"I'll take more painkiller. I'll grit my teeth. But do it."

Six hours later the tattoo was finished. The old man, beaming with satisfaction at his handiwork, with an extra thousand-dollar bonus in his hand, left.

Alvise had been standing by, brandy and other remedies, at his disposal, ready to minister to the moaning and crying man on the tattoo table. Somehow, Ciaccio bore through it all like a soldier. It is amazing what one will endure all in the name of love.

"Well, how do you like it?" Ciaccio asked Alvise when the old man left.

"Gorgeous. I've never seen anything like it in all my born days. The important question is, Will Rick like it?"

"He'll love it. And if he doesn't I'll hand him his head. Get me a mirror!"

Alvise brought a big one and held it up to Ciaccio's chest. Ciaccio was still crying, whether from the tattoo alone or in combination with deep feeling, it was impossible to tell.

"Incredible!" he whispered, scrutinizing himself in the mirror. "Rick wants a proof of love, this should do it."

The tattoo was magnificent. Rick's name in all six colors of the rainbow shone over the background—a rendering of the head of Saladin the Fierce, Ciaccio's trademark. As a border, all around the central image, amid rose petals and ivy leaves, the old man had engraved the Chinese ideogram for "love."

Putting aside the mirror, Ciaccio gingerly got up off the table, wincing over the pain of the fresh tattoo.

"It's time to get organized. I'll wait for him in the azure room—I'll wear my white satin coverall. You, meanwhile, will pick him up at the airport in the gray Rolls. Fill the back with hundreds of long-stemmed red roses. Bring him straight here. Every second will be an eternity until he's back in my arms."

"Have you considered playing a little hard to get—especially after all he put you through?"

Through the stabs of pain, Ciaccio smiled. "I love him even more now than before. There's nothing equal to the happiness of regaining a lost love. It's all part of the game."

Alvise thought Rick was ordinary street trash, but he kept his opinion to himself. He was still getting his piece of the pie. Besides, it was none of his business.

"I'd better be going," Alvise said.

Even though the codeine was wearing off, Ciaccio smiled bravely through his pain and waved, "Hurry, hurry. Rick doesn't like to be kept waiting."

* * *

If Rick Stanton was suffering at all from jet lag, he certainly wasn't showing it. Everyone else on his flight crawled off, hollow-eyed and stupefied. Rick emerged from the plane glowing and radiant, his tan perfect, his incredibly white teeth shining in his smiling face.

When they reached the Rolls, he gracefully picked up one red rose and held it to his nose. Sniffing it, he said, "Ah, Ciaccio's marvelous. He really has an old-fashioned sense of style."

For some reason, this put Alvise over the edge. He couldn't help saying, "Ciaccio deserves a lot better than you, that's all I know."

"Who asked you, anyway?" Rick said pleasantly.

"Have you any idea what an incredible mess you caused?"

"I can imagine. But Ciaccio deserved it. He treated me like an ingrate."

"You just got through saying he had style."

"The two are not mutually exclusive. He wants total devotion from me. But what does he offer in exchange? A few baubles, a gift here and there."

Thoroughly familiar with Ciaccio's finances, Alvise exploded. "A few baubles! Ciaccio spent close to fifty thousand dollars on you—and that's not counting the Porsche."

"Crumbs. I have to think of my future. In the last year, I've put on five pounds. This keeps up, I'll soon have a belly like yours. Then also, my father's bald and they say that kind of thing is hereditary. How long do you think Ciaccio would keep me if I pudge out and go bald? He'd find another Big Jim so fast I wouldn't have time to spit. That's why I insist on marrying his sister. I want security."

"You've thought it all out, haven't you?"

Alvise was beginning to feel a grudging sense of admiration for Rick—seeing it from Rick's point of view. He thought Rick was all facade; it turns out the guy has a brain or two in his head as well.

Alvise felt the need to probe. "Then you like women too?"

126

"In a manner of speaking. I've never had too much luck with them. I always seem to attract widows who have much too much time on their hands. That makes them possessive and penny-pinching. Ciaccio's different."

"How?"

"Ciaccio's not an idle widow with time on his hands. He's got a career, a big business to run. He's working all the time. That means he's less underfoot, not as demanding of me. I like having a lot of free time."

"So you can cause more mischief?" Alvise asked. "Because of you, we almost lost the new collection."

Rick said, "Calm down, Alvise. It's not in my nature to cause trouble. I like things to go along smoothly too. If Ciaccio sticks to his word, and I marry his sister, the waters will never be ruffled. I'll be the only man in his life and he'll be the only man in mine. Pure domestic bliss."

"That's just what I wanted to hear," Alvise said, relieved.

As they pulled up to the house, Alvise said, "Treat him nicely. He's gone through hell over you."

"O.K. Leave it all to me."

As Ciaccio saw Rick arrive and get out of the Rolls, he realized his legs were trembling. His heart was racing and his hands were clammy with cold sweat. For all his sophistication, Rick's reappearance reduced him to the level of an inexperienced teenager.

For one wild moment he panicked and thought of running off and hiding in the bathroom. But there was no time. Rick was approaching him, looking even more beautiful than Ciaccio remembered. He didn't think that was possible. He stood there trembling as Rick lifted a hand and gently caressed Ciaccio's face.

"Oh, Rick, you . . . " Rick put a hand over his lips.

"Sh. Don't say anything," Rick said as he put his arm around Ciaccio and kissed him lovingly on the mouth.

The kiss did it. Ciaccio melted. All the torment, all the resentment, all the fears were gone. Rick was back in his arms and, pressing himself up tight against Rick, he knew everything would be all right.

When they finally came up for air, Ciaccio's eyes were shining with happiness. "It's so great having you back home," he said.

"It's great for me too," Rick said. "I really missed you."

"If only you had come right out and told me what it was you wanted, we could have been spared all this unhappiness," Ciaccio murmured.

In response, Rick took his hand and kissed it lovingly. "There's no sense in talking about 'if only.' That's all in the past. Forget it, now that we have each other again."

Ciaccio disengaged his hand and reached up to undo the top part of his satin coveralls. He revealed the tattoo in all its multicolored glory.

Rick was stunned. He'd never seen anything remotely like it. "You did that for me?"

Ciaccio found himself blushing—was that possible? "I wanted to show by some token how much I love you."

"My God, talk about proof of love! Now I really understand how much you've gone through. I promise I'll never ever hurt you again."

Ciaccio was close to tears, tears of joy. "Let's go to bed. We have a busy day tomorrow."

"What's happening tomorrow?"

"We drive to the villa. Sabina will be there. We have to work out all the details of our—and I do mean our—wedding. Is that all right with you?"

Rick smiled and took his hand in his. "Just as long as we agree Till death do us part."

Ciaccio was overcome with emotion. "That's the most beautiful thing you ever said. Oh God, I love you, Rick!"

There were only the three of them at dinner the next day at the villa—Rick, Ciaccio and Sabina. The vast dining room echoed with their voices and the footsteps of the Vietnamese butler, the

French sommelier and the rest of the staff. Ciaccio sat at the head of the table in a black-velvet suit (a gift from Yves St. Laurent) and a gold Cartier chain around his neck. The atmosphere was thick with tension. Rick, in a light blue summer suit that set off his tan to perfection, had not said a word by the end of the meal when the fruit was served.

Sabina's way of dealing with the tension was the very opposite—she would not, or perhaps could not, stop talking. She babbled on indiscriminately about any subject that came to mind. If Ciaccio hadn't known better, he would have assumed she was flying on speed. But Sabina never used speed.

Rick had really taken to her. She was one of those women who didn't make much of an impression on first meeting, but over the course of time grew on one. He began to see a muted eroticism in her as well.

Sabina, on the other hand, never considered Rick anything more than a handsome gigolo, subcategory: California blond. But here, in the villa, his eroticism was beginning to work on her and she was having a change of mind. Besides his good looks, he was soft-spoken, well-mannered and considerate. As a husband—albeit pro forma—he would not embarrass her in public. His looks would guarantee her the envy of all her friends. Of course none of them would know that she was merely the skirt—the female coverup for Rick's liaison with her brother.

When dinner was over, Ciaccio stood up and said, "Shall we adjourn to the library for coffee?"

Sabina said, "You know I never drink coffee."

Ciaccio smiled at his sister. "You mustn't be so literal, Sabina. I was speaking generically, so to speak." He always felt paternalistically indulgent toward her. She had no ambitions, no head for business. Having as good a time as was possible was her *raison d'être*. Ciaccio had never minded supporting her. Now, surprisingly, she would serve a useful purpose in a way he never would have foreseen. He was also grateful she had broken off with that child molester she'd been engaged to.

129

They all walked into the library. Sabina smiled at Rick, he smiled back. He really is gorgeous, she thought. I'm beginning to understand the fascination he holds for Ciaccio.

Once the various aperitifs were poured and the snifters handed about, they got down to business. Ciaccio said, "I think the marriage should be as soon as possible."

"What about the engagement announcement?" Sabina asked.

Ciaccio said, "It doesn't have to be super-official. We can have a modest engagement party. Followed by a modest romantic wedding in a little provincial church somewhere."

Sabina held up her hand as if to say, Go no further. "I'm sorry, Ciaccio. I can do without a big brouhaha of an engagement. But I want a big, big wedding." Here she smiled at Rick. "We Catholics marry once and it's for life. It's my only chance. I want the wedding at San Babila." San Babila was one of the biggest churches in Milan.

Ciaccio looked at Rick. "What do you think?"

"I have no objections. I don't mind the publicity—as long as the bride is happy." He smiled at Sabina.

Ciaccio said, "If that's what Sabina really wants, and you don't mind the publicity . . . "

"There's nothing wrong with publicity," Rick said.

Like Mittaglia before her, Sabina was pleasantly surprised at Rick's astuteness. Since it was so often the case that very beautiful people were also very stupid, an exception like Rick was that much more refreshing.

"That's settled, then. You'll have your wedding at San Babila. What else do you want, Sabina?"

"A villa on the Emerald Coast, an apartment in Cortina, a Ferrari Testa Rosa and a Bentley, and the apartment I now have in Milan."

"I see you've given the subject some thought," Ciaccio said wryly.

"I also want one million dollars transferred to my Swiss account and an annuity of five thousand dollars a month for life."

Rick glanced at Sabina, admiration in his eyes. Even Ciaccio was surprised and impressed at Sabina's canny list of demands. "It's apparent you gave your list a lot of thought, signorina," Rick said.

"Call me Sabina. After all, we're almost husband and wife—at least on paper."

"Fine by me, Sabina."

"Well, I'm glad that's all settled," Ciaccio said.

"What do you mean?" Rick asked. "You still haven't heard my list."

"I thought that was your joint list—community property and all that."

"Not by a long shot. For starters, I want a high-level executive position with Irone Fashions. I've got great ideas and I want to be able to put them into practice. I also want ten percent of the shares in the corporation. This is a great deal for you, Ciaccio— my ideas will double your turnover in no time."

Ciaccio's thinking wasn't exactly along the same lines as Rick's. Rick's proposal of an executive position simply meant that Ciaccio would be spending all his days with his beloved as well as his nights.

He looked at his sister. "What do you think, Sabina?"

"I go along with Rick. I think you lucked out on the deal."

Ciaccio announced, "Mittaglia will draw up both your contracts tonight and we can sign them in front of a notary tomorrow. How's that?"

"Now's the time for champagne," she said. She rang for the butler and in no time they were toasting each other with Taittinger's finest.

After a sip, Sabina looked up and asked Ciaccio, "Am I permitted to have men on the side?"

"Of course," Ciaccio agreed. "You can have donkeys on the side—if you're discreet."

She then turned to Rick. "Is that all right with you?"

Rick smiled. "Donkeys? Sure. As long as you're discreet and

131

word doesn't get about. I value my reputation."

"Spoken like a true man," she said. "I assure you *if* I play around, I will be discretion itself."

"In that case," Rick said, lifting his glass in a toast, "Here's to the happiest couple in Milan."

Ciaccio beamed on them both, happy they were getting along so well. Fortunately he was not privy to their thoughts.

Chapter 14

*P*asqualetta Amiani would not settle for being ugly. No one denied she was ugly, in fact, she was the first one in any group to mention it. Her ugliness, however, had a certain distinction. She was memorably unattractive. Nothing was "right" about her face, which to the right connoisseur's eyes made her fascinating. She, on the other hand, saw only the ugliness, not its special distinction. By the time she was 45, she had had a Swiss facelift, and three sessions with Elio Oldrini and was soon planning to go to Rio to the great Pitanguy for further plastic surgery.

She was immensely intelligent—ain't it the way—and was editor-in-chief of *Highlife*, the most beautiful fashion magazine in the world. Needless to say, her position was one of great power. Directors come and go, but the editor-in-chief lasts forever.

Highlife was in a class by itself. True, there was *Chic*, whose editor Giffo Santarelli wanted to believe was as formidable in the marketplace, but the truth of the matter was that *Highlife* ruled the fashion world. What it decreed was law. Like as not it was Pasqualetta who issued the decrees.

Moving through a world populated by international beauties was what demoralized Pasqualetta. Every new beautiful face she took as a personal rebuke.

Pasqualetta was very aware of her ability to wield power. She had a near insatiable appetite for handsome young men, one that could only be fulfilled by lavishing huge sums of money on them. This Pasqualetta did not have. Nevertheless, she did very well for herself, all things considered. She had something even more persuasive than a checkbook—power. To get on her bad side was to commit career suicide. Her ability to wield power and influence had drawn many a young man into her embrace in a way, perhaps, not even a lot of money would have.

She knew perfectly well that it wasn't her charisma or charm that kept her bed populated. She never deceived herself on that score. She was not looking for romance, she was in the market for temporary satisfaction. And that she got completely. Everybody knew that one word from her could make or break a model's career.

Ugo Varanni called her at her office. This put her immediately on her guard. She was in no doubt as to his character. Nevertheless, he'd been of help to her in the past.

She picked up the phone and without even saying hello, she said, "If you're looking for a loan, Varanni, forget it."

"I don't need money, Pasqualetta," he replied. "I merely want to introduce you to a friend of mine."

"What's he like?"

"In three hours. At Emilio's."

Hanging up, Pasqualetta was grateful he picked that out-of-the-way joint. She'd die if anyone caught her in public with such a lowlife as Varanni.

I wonder what he's got up his sleeve, she thought as she fixed her makeup in her compact mirror.

"I have to go somewhere," she told Priscilla, her secretary, as she headed for the door.

"Any idea when you'll be back?"

"There's no way of telling. It's pretty slow today. If I don't come back until tomorrow, you know what to say."

"What if a crisis arises?"

"You know there's no such thing as a crisis in magazine publishing." They both had a good laugh over that one.

"Have fun!"

Calvin was on his third whiskey.

"Hey, go easy on that stuff. Don't forget. You have a performance coming up soon."

"Drink only seems to affect my ballplaying, not my fucking. In fact, I think it helps my fucking."

"Now don't say I didn't warn you. This woman is no raving beauty."

"For a thousand bucks, I'd fuck a snake—if I could find the hole. While we're on the subject, where's my money?"

Varanni handed him a check.

"I want cash—no one in Milan will cash a check from you."

"It's a teller's check. It's as good as cash."

"Why didn't you just bring cash?"

"Because this way, if you renege, I can always stop the check."

"I won't renege."

"Maybe the lady won't be satisfied."

"I don't want to brag, but if I fuck them, they're satisfied. Take bets on it."

Calvin stood nearly seven feet tall and had an immensely well-proportioned body. His face was no less than stunning. All the women (straight) and men (gay) in the restaurant had been eyeing him since he and Varanni had entered.

Calvin had arrived in Milan four years ago to join a basketball team. He was a rising star until he had his collision with the bottle. As the booze went down into him, his career went down the drain. There wasn't a night that went by that didn't see him in a new stupor—maybe it was one long stupor. His drinking led to public brawls and when the team owners got tired bailing him out of fixes, they gave him the heave ho. Since then he'd been financing his habit by a little hustling here and there. He had heard of a guru who could miraculously cure his alcoholism and Varanni's thousand dollars was his one-way ticket to India and the miracle cure.

Pasqualetta entered, wearing dark glasses. "There she is," Varanni said.

"You must be kidding."

"You want to back out now?"

"I need the bucks."

Pasqualetta meanwhile had been eyeing Calvin. What she saw, she approved of. Varanni got up to join her. "Wait here," he said to Calvin.

"Can I have another drink?"

"From here on in it had better be Pepsi on the rocks."

Pasqualetta sat at a table in the back. Varanni joined her. "Well," he asked, "what do you think?"

"Right up my alley. If he can perform . . . "

"Take my word for it. You won't be able to walk straight for a week."

"Are you sure he won't try any fast ones—like blackmail, say?"

"Have you ever had problems with any of the bozos I set you up with?"

"In all truth, no. But stories from others have gotten around. It's time to put your cards on the table, Varanni. What exactly do you want in return? If you want me to launch one of your models, I can tell you right now it won't be easy. Your reputation stinks in this town."

"I admit I have an image problem, but I'll take care of that some other time. Right now I have another project going. I want from you the names of at least ten models now working for Diovisi. Their real names and addresses."

136

Pasqualetta squinted up her eyes in suspicion. "What kind of scam are you in to?"

"None of your business. If you help me, my friend over there—" With a gesture he indicated Calvin.

"O.K. Don't get your balls in an uproar. I have no intention of passing up such a hunk. But Diovisi's my friend . . ."

"I'm your friend too. And I guarantee your name will never be involved."

"All day and all night."

"What was that?"

"He's got to last all through the night into the morning."

"Are you in for a surprise!"

"It had better be a pleasant one."

"When can I get those names?"

"Tomorrow. If all goes well." She lit a cigarette and walked over to the black man. They exchanged a few words, then he got up and they left together.

Everything was going great. Last night Varanni had won 20 million liras at Campione. And now Pasqualetta would fall into line. God's in his heaven, all's right with the world.

One more detail to iron out. He'd have to contact Lo Porro at police headquarters. Lo Porro had the smelliest feet in Italy—it must be some kind of disease. Varanni was willing to overlook any amount of smelly feet to get this plan into action.

Adelio Lo Porro was coming off his shift. Milan's heat was blistering. He wished he was back in his native Calabria, bathing in the ocean. Most of the city's cops were on vacation. They were on a skeleton staff. Two years earlier Lo Porro had been caught with his fingers in the cookie jar—a juicy prostitution scandal—and so he was sweating out his probation, literally. His vacation wasn't until October.

Lo Porro was held by the short hairs by Varanni. Somehow Varanni had found out he, Lo Porro, was on the take of a secret gambling club in Milan. Lo Porro, already on probation, didn't want to take the risk of having the other shoe drop. So, whenever Varanni snapped his fingers, Lo Porro fetched.

Varanni caught Lo Porro just as he was leaving police headquarters.

"How's tricks?" Varanni asked.

"I'm fine. How are you?"

"I didn't realize you could be so witty, Lo Porro."

"Skip the chin music. What do you want, Varanni?"

"There's a girl—"

"Do you mean a girl or a woman? The women's libbers are getting on our backs about that."

"Correction. There's a young woman I want arrested and I want you to do it."

"What did she do?"

"You're missing the point. I don't want her really arrested. I want her scared, submissive, docile. You'll need some help I would think."

"Let me worry about that. Who is she?"

"I'll give you her name and all her particulars tomorrow. Can I count on you?"

"Think of me as an abacus."

"Hey you are getting witty. How's your feet?"

"I've tried everything. There's no help."

"Ah, but have you tried washing with soap and water?"

Lo Porro turned his back and walked away.

Stop the presses! An unprecedented event had occurred. Pasqualetta's appetite for sex had been sated—totally sated. All afternoon, into the evening, into the late evening, into the night, through the night Calvin had been hammering away at her and it was *she*, at about dawn, who said, "I can't take any more. You'll have to stop." It was the first time *ever* in a career filled with all-night marathon couplings that she was the one to blow the whistle. Her body would eventually recover, but the blow to her ego, to her sense of self should be longer lasting. Was this a sign of the inevitable approach of age?

It was now ten A.M. They'd gotten a little sleep and he was now in the bathroom showering. She hobbled into the bathroom to watch as the water cascaded over that extraordinary body—a veritable engine of pleasure.

Later, drying him off with a big fluffy towel, as she was patting his genitalia dry and causing it to stir once again to vibrant life, she said, awash in admiration, "You're still hot to trot, aren't you?"

Calvin hit his chest in a Tarzan-like tattoo with his fists. "I'm always in the mood for love. You want to go another inning?"

Pasqualetta shivered at the very thought. "God, no. As it is, I'll probably be limping for a week. However . . . " She stammered, shy as an inexperienced teenager. "If you'd like to come back some other time . . . I'd love to take you on again . . . I could even give you a present or two . . . "

Calvin shook his head no. "Not on your life. I'm getting on a plane out of here and I'm not coming back. Thanks for the compliment though."

"Is there anything I can do for you?"

"You could put up some coffee."

After coffee, he left and Pasqualetta crawled back into bed. She lay there running over the night before on the VCR of her mind, instant replaying some of the highlights. She was moaning with remembered pleasure.

The phone rang. It was Varanni. "How's the publishing queen of Milan's fashion industry this fine morning?" he asked.

"Could not be better. Every morning after should be like this."

"No cause for complaints?"

"Are you kidding? He was fabulous. By the way, what was his name?"

"Didn't you ask?"

"We had no time for small talk."

"His name was Calvin. Changing the subject, how about a little business talk?"

"If you insist. But it sure is hard readjusting to the world of logic and reason after last night. When do you need the names?"

"Is half an hour too soon?"

"Don't rush me. You'll have them by three this afternoon."

"Leave the names in an envelope with the receptionist at *Highlife*. I'll pick it up."

"I'd rather you send someone else. I'm uncomfortable with the idea of your being seen there at all."

"Fine. I'll send someone. Thanks, Pasqualetta."

He was a nervous wreck, pacing up and down. What could have delayed her? He had sent Giovanna to pick up the envelope and she should have been back long ago. He poured himself another whiskey—his third of the afternoon. If Giovanna fucks this up in any way, he thought, I'll take it out of her ass.

At last, he heard a key in the front door. It was Giovanna.

"I'm sorry I took so long, *caro*. It took forever to find a cab."

"O.K. O.K. Where's the envelope?"

She fished it out of her purse. He practically tore it in two ripping it out of her grasp.

"I had no idea it was so important. Is it a check?"

"It's not a check," Varanni said as he ripped open the envelope and extracted one typewritten sheet of paper. It was a list of models, Diovisi's stable this season.

The bottom name on the list struck a familiar note. Jenny Moore from Detroit. Pseudonym: Sarah. There was a phone number as well.

Looking over his shoulder, Giovanna was puzzled more than anything else. "What's this all about?" she asked timidly.

"Just a model list. Incidentally, do you remember a Barbie from Detroit named Jenny Moore? Wasn't she at our agency last year for a little while?"

"Jennie Moore, Jennie Moore. Let me think. Yes, of course, I remember her. Pretty little thing, but such a prude, so straight-laced. I remember her well. Why do you ask?"

"She's come up in the world, doing well for herself. She no longer calls the Princess Clithilde her home. Has a nice address now."

"What's it to us?"

"I'd like you to give her a call. Ask her to meet you."

Giovanna said, "*Caro*, if a model has risen in the world, she's not going to come back to an agency like ours."

"Call her anyway. See if you can set up an appointment for tonight."

"I can give it a try."

"Tell her it's in her own best interests. Make up something. Say there's a letter for her from Detroit. Do anything necessary, but get her to meet you."

"Ugo, something smells fishy. What are you up to anyway?"

"It may not seem so now, but this could be our big break. No more dunning letters or threatening notices from the phone company."

"Why do I have this odd feeling in the pit of my stomach?"

"Take an Alka-Seltzer. You'll feel better. Now call Jenny."

Chapter 15

Fuxia Taylor was in a down mood, and when she was down, she was way down. Inna was the cause of it all. At first, Fuxia wanted to blame Inna's aunt, Diana Rau, for unduly influencing her niece, but it just wasn't the case. After Inna's bout with the coke overdose she had moved out of the apartment she'd shared with Fuxia and was now living with her aunt. But it wasn't just that Inna had moved out of Fuxia's apartment—she'd moved out of her life. She no longer called—there was no contact between them at all. Fuxia was so down, because it had hit her full force that enjoying Fuxia and sharing her bed was merely a pleasant pastime to Inna. For Fuxia, Inna was the sun and moon and stars. She had no idea how deeply she was in love with Inna herself until the affair was already over.

Like all spurned lovers, Fuxia wouldn't believe the affair was really over. If it meant taking the blame for something, for anything, she would do it just so she could be with Inna again.

Although in her heart she realized it was futile, Fuxia reached for the phone and dialed Inna's number.

"Hello."

It was Inna.

"Hello, Inna. It's Fuxia." Her heart was racing.

"Oh yes, how have you been?" Cool, dispassionate.

"Inna, I have to see you. I have to talk to you."

"Is it about some work?"

Inna was scarcely cordial. She certainly didn't sound encouraging.

Fuxia was clutching at straws. "Yes, that too. Oh Inna, I've missed you so much."

"To be perfectly frank, Fuxia, I haven't missed you at all. You were beginning to become a real drag."

"But Inna, *cara*, I love you."

"Are you still singing that tune? Don't you realize there's no hope for our having any kind of relationship?"

"I'll do anything, as long as you'll let me see you, touch you, be near you. If you want to, you can bring home guys, I won't mind. Please, my darling."

"Don't be such a bore."

"Can I see you tonight?"

"I'm going to say it once so listen up. I don't want to see you ever again."

"But why? What have I done? Is it something I said?"

"It's everything in general. I'm bored with you. It's all over."

"But we were so good together."

"Fuxia, I'm not going to beat around the bush."

"Tell me, what is it really?"

"You're bad luck, Fuxia. You're one of those people who trail disaster wherever they go. Bad news."

"But Inna . . . "

But Inna had hung up.

Fuxia was now in a towering rage. How blind Inna was. How

stupidly superstitious. Can people really be that gullible? So she was bad luck, was she? We'll see about that, she thought. She would get all dolled up and go out on the town tonight. The first person she met who knocked on wood or crossed his fingers, she'd scratch their eyes out for them. She *would* be bad news.

She had to fuel up properly for such an evening. One speedball coming up—the combination of whiskey, aspirin and coke was the right prescription for tonight.

Her brain was free associating. She recalled John, her first lover, before she had discovered women. He had been killed in a car crash. Then she remembered her roommate in New York when she was first starting out—dead from an overdose—the needle still in her arm. Then there was Mark, the photographer who discovered her. Suicide. No one ever understood why. He had everything to live for.

The speedball was ricocheting through her nervous system. She could feel herself getting taut and edgy. So what if I'm really a jinx, she thought as she was getting dressed. Fuck them, fuck them all.

She called for a cab. She studied herself in the mirror until he arrived. She had never been so beautiful.

Paolo Sgargaglia was at loose ends. Sardinia had turned into an island of ribbon clerks. Monte Carlo was even hotter than Milan. He needed to meet someone new. Someone exciting. Milan would serve as well as anyplace else. He had a reputation as a cocksman to uphold.

He had the biggest Rolodex of any Don Juan in Italy. It was per capita the longest list of European beauties this side of Leporello's. If there was one thing Paolo hated it was screwing the same woman more than three times. His favorite maxim, which had once circulated throughout Milan, was: "The first time, to break the ice. The second time, to find out whether you like the girl. And the third time, to enjoy. Anything after that is a waste of time."

That evening, he had been at the Caffe Roma, then Charlie Max, and finally Baretto. But he hadn't seen anyone outside the usual faces. The usual top models, the usual gourmet diners, the usual deadbeats and moochers. Paolo had elegantly fended them off and immediately returned to his adored Rolls-Royce.

Now, he was listlessly hanging around the bar of the Nepentha.

"I'm bored out of my skull," he announced to the bartender, who, for lack of other customers, was listening very attentively.

At that moment, he noticed two so-so broads among the ones who had just walked in. They were both gazing at him with avid interest. They must have recognized him from recent photos in newspapers. Two weeks ago, he had been shown with Barbara Bouchet . . . Or was it Edwige Fenech? Paolo couldn't remember precisely. He only recalled that he had sent for the paparazzo the afternoon the movie star had asked him to go shopping with her. It had cost him five hundred bucks. But nobody would ever find out that he had paid the guy. Or that he hadn't even grazed the star's arm. He had trailed along for two incredibly boring hours, always addressing her as "ma'am" and he had finally dropped her at her hotel.

The important thing was that the next day he could experience the vicarious thrill, as now, of being pointed to by strangers. Reflected glory was still a kind of glory.

He really was quite handsome. And because he always wore shoes with reinforced heels, no one was aware of how short he really was—except him. His long curly hair haloed around his head making him seem even taller somehow. He loved his Rolls-Royce. He loved being thought of as a lover of international beauties. The first love was consummated a lot more often than the second.

Referring to the women who had so recently been pointing at him, he said to the bartender, "They ought to turn this place into a private club. What they let in these days is depressingly the wrong element."

Humoring him, the bartender said, "I'll speak to the manager about it."

Paolo was drowning in boredom. When he reviewed his options, he was even more depressed. He could drive over to Lugano to see Dolly or Sophia or over to Bologna for some late-night pasta primavera or he could just drive around in his Rolls for hours aimlessly until he wore himself out.

He left the bar and had just gotten into the driver's seat when he saw Fuxia, beautiful and elegantly dressed, emerge from a cab and head into the bar.

It all came back. He remembered her. Several weeks ago he had seen her and a girlfriend take on five men at once and come out the victors.

She had stuck in his mind, although he wasn't one of the five. For one thing, she was American and he had a real fondness for Americans. When it came to sex, they were the most fun—so open-minded, so willing to try something new. Maybe it was because they all went to shrinks. He couldn't figure out the connection why talking about one's psyche lying down in a shrink's office liberated it when lying down in a stranger's bed, but he was sure the connection existed.

Further, he had heard that Fuxia was essentially a lesbian, the thought of which, at least, he found to be a great turn on.

Hadn't he heard something else? Whatever it was, it slipped his mind. It would come to him later.

He got out of the Rolls and returned to the bar. The bartender didn't blink an eye.

Fuxia was sitting at a table and talking to Bubi Fallaci. Bubi ran a china factory during the day and ran himself ragged all night. His defect was a serious one: he kept falling in love. He wasn't satisfied until he felt he really *loved* a woman—not liked, that wasn't enough—before he would make his move. Invariably by this time the woman had given up and taken off for greener pastures. Paolo made his mind up—that night he would steal the Barbie away from Bubi.

Bubi was yammering away about something but Fuxia wasn't

paying attention. The effect of the speedball was wearing off and her thoughts had returned to Inna. She could feel the tears welling up in her eyes.

She had some coke and some aspirin in her purse. With not too much difficulty she poured the aspirin into her whiskey. But she would need the privacy of the women's bathroom to do the coke. She noticed Paolo at the bar and tried to place where she knew him from. There was something about him that rubbed her the wrong way. Instant dislike. If she could only remember where she'd met him before. No matter. She gulped down the aspirin-spiked whiskey and stood up abruptly. Bubi was in mid-sentence.

"Hey, where are you going?"

"I have to go to the bathroom."

"You go ahead. I'll tell you about my place in Portofino when you get back."

"Excuse me," she said as she stumbled toward the women's bathroom.

Paolo had seen her go off to the bathroom, of course. After several minutes, and she still hadn't returned, he decided to see what was the matter.

He opened the door quietly and gently. There was Fuxia leaning against the wall, near the sink, a little telltale white powder giving her something like a white mustache.

Even better, he thought. This way, she won't put up much of a struggle. Suddenly he recalled the other detail about her he'd heard—she was a jinx.

Although Paolo prided himself on being not in the least superstitious, he was also nobody's fool. Just to make sure as he approached Fuxia, he touched his balls.

Looking in the mirror, Fuxia noticed his gesture—the Italian male version of crossing his fingers. She spun around and glared at him.

"Do you think I'm bad luck?"

"I was just scratching myself. I think something about you all right, but not that."

148

"What?"

"I think you're a very sexy woman. I'd love to make love to you."

"Go fuck yourself, shrimp."

She had touched on his most vulnerable point. He grabbed hold of her arm roughly. "If I fuck anyone, it'll be you, Barbie."

"Let go of my arm."

"Come along nicely now."

"Let go, I say."

Paolo clutched her even harder. "The last time I saw you, you were fucking a small army. You and your friend."

"Inna," Fuxia sighed.

"That's the one. She wasn't as beautiful as you."

The memory of that night rose up in Fuxia's mind. All of a sudden she wanted to be away from all this—far away.

The second speedball hadn't hit yet. She put up a struggle but the bastard wouldn't let go of her arm. She clawed at his face—she made two deep bloody gashes along his left cheek. This gave her an immense sense of satisfaction.

He slammed her in the face, knocking her to the floor. Her head banged against the foot of the sink. She lay there, stunned.

She saw him shift his weight back onto his left foot. She could see he was preparing to kick her. She wanted to scream but she was frozen with fear.

Suddenly, he pulled out his cock and said, "I don't need you after all."

Hovering over her, he began to jack off. He shifted his weight so that he held her on the floor with his foot on her chest. He was approaching climax, she could tell.

Finally he came. She had tried to shift position just as he was doing so and with satisfaction she noticed much of his come had splattered onto the front of his slacks.

"Are you finished?" she asked disdainfully.

"Not quite yet."

"Oh yes you are." This came from Bubi who had just peeked

in out of concern for Fuxia's long absence.

"This doesn't concern you," Paolo said.

"Wrong again. She's with me." Before Paolo could say anything else, Bubi had pulled him off her and had him pinned to the wall.

"How can you date such trash?" Paolo asked.

That did it. Bubi's fist smashed into Paolo's chin and he was reeling from the blow. All this over a jinx, no less, Paolo thought. Paolo started hitting back. He landed a couple of good ones in Bubi's side. Taking advantage of the brawl, Fuxia tidied herself as hurriedly and as best she could and ran back into the bar. Stopping at her table momentarily to pick up her cigarettes and lighter, she noticed Bubi's car keys. She grabbed them and ran outside. She remembered Bubi had mentioned he drove a Land Rover. A Land Rover may not be the height of chic, but it is distinctively and easily identifiable.

There was a Land Rover—the only one on the block—parked in front of the bar. She hopped in. Her one thought was to get away, not just away from the bar, but away from Milan, away from Italy, perhaps to go back to America.

She switched into first gear and was about to pull away when she noticed the Rolls-Royce parked nearby. Paolo's reputation had both preceded and followed him. She remembered all the stories she'd heard about him and his Rolls. By now she was feeling no pain, thanks to the speedball.

A knowing smile appeared on Fuxia's lips. She knew how she'd retaliate, how she would pay Paolo back for his humiliating her in the bathroom.

She pulled into the road, reversed and shifted into first, then smashed into the side of the Rolls.

Once again, reverse, first, then full speed ahead until she smashed into the Rolls again.

She kept repeating the procedure. At one point a few people gathered on the sidewalk to watch, but no one made a move to stop her.

150

Finally the Rolls was totalled. Feeling a lot better, Fuxia pulled away and drove off into the night.

Chapter 16

Italy was not as highly evolved, not anywhere near so sophisticated as, say, Sweden. In Sweden, it was legal for a brother to marry his sister. It was legal for a group of three people to marry each other. It was legal to marry two people of the same sex. In Italy, that was not even to be considered. How Ciaccio would have loved to be married *legally* to Rick. Sabina would have to be his proxy, there was no other way. And of course, he should have predicted that, Sabina being Sabina, she would want the grandest wedding imaginable.

Things were moving ahead, back on schedule. As soon as Rick had returned, Ciaccio's creative juices started flowing full force and his new collection was a knockout. Rick, home from his escape—or escapade—was in his arms every night providing love and inspiration.

Ciaccio was immensely pleased with the way things were

turning out. Right that minute, Rick and Sabina were formally applying for the marriage license at City Hall. The banns would be published the next day and in a few weeks the marriage would be a *fait accompli*. People might have their suspicions, but they would never know the truth. Though the marriage of Rick and Sabina would be a farce, no one would be any the wiser.

The phone rang. It was Sabina.

"It's done, Ciaccio. I was so moved. For a moment there it felt like it was real."

"Where's Rick?"

"He went to the U.S. Consulate to get some documents. I'm calling from a bar nearby."

"As soon as he returns send him back to me at once. I have a couple of things I need to talk to him about."

"I'm sorry, brother dearest. But we have other plans."

Was that twinge he felt a twinge of jealousy by any chance? "Why? What do you mean you have other plans? What about . . . "

"Calm down, Ciaccio. I simply felt it was time to introduce my fiancé to some of my friends. If I didn't it would start to seem suspicious. They're all dying to meet him. Don't worry. Tonight I'll send him back to you, safe and sound."

"O.K. Don't make it too late—I'm keeping early hours these days."

After he hung up, Ciaccio realized how reasonable Sabina was being. If she was engaged to be married, of course she would be anxious to introduce her prospective husband to all her friends. Anything less would surely cause gossip.

He returned to the mountains of sketches he had been studying before she called. Was there anything between Sabina and Rick, anything, that is, more than what met the eye?

Rick had been at the consulate. He couldn't believe how much red tape there was in the simple act of marrying abroad. He was wearing a jacket and tie. He felt the visit to get the license and

154

then the trip to the consulate demanded dressing up. He was sweating profusely by the time he turned up in the bar, but somehow it made him look even more handsome than ever. He approached Sabina's table, sat down and smiled.

"It was complex, but I think everything that needs to be is ironed out at the consulate. Did you call Ciaccio?"

"A couple of minutes ago, in fact. He seems very happy these days."

"Why shouldn't he be? Everything's working out for him. Did he want me back this afternoon?"

"As a matter of fact, he suggested you take the rest of the afternoon off. How about we drive somewhere and have a picnic?"

"Sounds fine by me."

"If you like, maybe later we could stop by my place for a light supper."

He seemed to be catching on to some level of vibration. He looked her in the eyes and said, "We could leave right now if you like."

Sabina felt a tingle of desire rush over her. Rick had caught on. And he was seemingly willing. She patted herself on the back mentally for being so clever in working this out. Last night, almost on a whim, she had borrowed the key to a friend's pied-à-terre. It was her own special tricking pad—her husband knew about it, but pretended not to. Sabina was afraid to do anything in her own home. Servants were great gossipers. This nuptial ménage-à-trois was a great windfall for her and she had no intention of stupidly fucking it up by making a wrong move.

As they got into the car, she asked, "What if Ciaccio finds out?"

"I won't say anything. If you won't say anything, we're safe."

After driving along for a bit in silence, Sabina said, "Are you sure this is all right with you?"

"Our having sex? Would you rather show me your stamp collection?"

Sabina laughed. "Not quite. But I don't want to force the

155

issue."

Rick didn't answer. Instead he reached over and took Sabina's right hand and placed it over his groin. He held her hand there. She could feel him starting to grow hard.

"How's that for an answer?"

"Decisive. Unequivocal." She was beginning to get wet herself. After a pause, she asked, "Does Ciaccio turn you on?"

"Don't be foolish. Of course he does."

Sabina turned a corner and pulled up. "Here we are!"

Rick glanced around. "You don't live around here."

"Merely a detail. There's an air-conditioned apartment and there's a bed. What more do we need?"

The apartment's atmosphere was close—the air conditioner was too small for the space it had to cool.

Sabina was lying back in a state of sated exhaustion. She had worked up a real sweat, but somehow she didn't seem to mind. Rick had lived up to her hopes—far exceeding her expectations. He was passionate. He was creative. And he was very nearly indefatigable.

When they'd first arrived, she'd said, "Close your eyes and leave everything to me." He closed his eyes as instructed. She undressed him and led him to the bed. She made him lie down on his back and proceeded to give him a long and thorough tongue bath. Several times she had brought him to the threshold of orgasm and then pulled away.

Finally she couldn't hold off any longer and she got on top of him and straddled him. "Ride 'em, cowgirl!" he called out.

She didn't seem to hear him, already lost in the whirlpool of her own sexuality. The biggest surprise—even greater than Rick's expertise—was her own powerful response. Sex, till now, had been a pleasant plaything, something to while away idle hours. This time, she found herself swept up into a tornado of sensuality that left her breathless and a little bit dizzy. She'd never felt anything like this with Carlo Venanzi, but then again she now

156

knew she wasn't his type. She also now knew he hadn't been hers.

Collapsed on the bed, she stretched like a cat. A future vision of many afternoons like this spent with her "husband" brought a smug grin to her face. Ciaccio would be none the wiser, of course.

Rick had just finished showering. Instead of toweling himself dry he came into the bedroom, naked and dripping, and placed himself in front of the vents of the air conditioner. His penis, completely relaxed, hung majestically. It seemed to be wearing him. Sabina mentally saluted Ciaccio for his exquisite taste in men.

"Come back to bed," she called out.

"Are you still horny?"

"It's all your fault. I had no idea sex with you would be so great."

"Are you developing a taste for gay men?"

"How can you say you're gay after that performance! At the least you're bisexual. You told me yourself you go with men because they're not so possessive as women—it has nothing to do with the sex act."

"That may well be, but I'd rather not talk about it."

"Fine by me, lover. Come here by me," she said as she patted the unoccupied part of the bed.

Rick lay down next to her and she began to lick the drops of water beading on his chest. He had taken a cold shower, and the cool water on his caramel-colored skin tasted heavenly to her.

While kissing his chest and licking his nipples, her hand had slowly stolen down to his pubic region. She was delighted—and proud—to discover he was hard again. She started scrunching down toward it on the bed.

"Do you feel up to it?" she asked.

Moving her head onto his cock, he said, "How's that for an answer?"

"How lucky Ciaccio is in having you in his bed every night."

"Why'd you have to bring him up now?"

"It just occurred to me, that's all."

She was now licking him in long strokes, from the base of his cock all the way to the tip, where she lingered a bit before making her descent.

"Yeah, that's it!" Rick encouraged her. "That's great!"

"Am I as good as my brother?"

"As a matter of fact, no. His technique's much better. Why do you have to ask questions like that anyhow? You're good. Now shut up and enjoy the moment."

Sabina did just that. All of a sudden they heard a key in the lock of the entrance to the next room. Sabina sat up. Rick froze, his smile disappearing. He looked scared. "Who can that be?" he asked. "Were you expecting someone?"

"Of course not, it's a friend's place."

The same thought occurred to them then—Ciaccio had had them followed. They had jeopardized it all for a quick afternoon of torrid sex. What a high price to pay for getting one's rocks off.

Sabina was the first to relax—she heaved a sigh of relief as she realized the footsteps were made by someone in high heels. That ruled out Ciaccio at least.

"Who is that?" she called out.

Her friend had appeared in the doorway. "It's just me, Elena."

Sabina and Rick farcically reached for the same end of the same blanket to cover their nudity. He won.

"I'm really so sorry to intrude," Elena said, not looking in the least bit sorry. She was eating Rick up with her eyes. "I didn't think anyone would be here."

There's always proper manners for any occasion. Taking a rather formal tone, Sabina said, "May I introduce Mr. Rick Stanton, my fiancé. Rick, this is an old friend of mine, Elena Balducci."

The two of them had no choice but to pick up the cue. Elena reached over and shook hands with Rick. "Nice to meet you," they both said.

Although Elena was smiling at Rick's face, it was also apparent she was not totally uninterested in another part of his anatomy that was hinted at under the tip of the blanket he was

158

clutching.

"I'm sorry about the air conditioner. It's really inadequate for this place," she said, fumbling for the right kind of small talk to make.

Sabina, unsure herself where this strange conversation was leading, if anywhere, began to feel uneasy. "It's getting sort of late. We ought to be going," she said as she reached over Rick for the end of the blanket he was not using.

"Don't be silly," Elena said. "Stay right where you are. It's really my fault after all. I'm the intruder. Can I get you something cool to drink?" Elena decided she would be hostess—a role she could slip into easily. Her real aim, none too well hidden from the others, was to slip into bed with them.

Sabina looked at Rick and tried to evaluate the situation. She hadn't partaken in much three-way sex in her life but that was more because the opportunity hadn't arisen very often, rather for any intrinsic dislike she might feel at the idea. But she had no idea how Rick felt on the matter. Also, it wasn't as if he was just someone she'd picked up off the street—he was her fiancé. This story would eventually get around and if Ciaccio ever got wind of it, her goose was cooked. Rick's too.

Rick's face was unfathomable. He said, "I could certainly use a cool drink right now."

"How's vodka and grapefruit juice?" Elena asked, getting into a party spirit. "I could do with a drink. And I'm all alone in the city. My husband's in the hospital with prostatitis and my boyfriend's with his folks in Rome." Leaving the room to get the drinks, she said, "I'll be back in a jiffy."

"Listen, Sabina, I don't want to hurt your feelings—or for that matter Elena's, she's very beautiful—but I've got to bow out on this one."

"Is it possible you have a streak of prudery deep within you?" she asked, more than a little surprised.

"You don't know me well enough to understand. Let me try and explain before she returns. I signed a contract with you and

159

Ciaccio. That's giving my word. Maybe I'm very old-fashioned, but when I give my word that's it. I promised Ciaccio he would be the only man in my life and I can promise you that you'll be the only woman. And you can sleep easy at night because I'll keep that promise. Any other arrangement is too complex, too devious for my taste. I want you to understand because I don't want to hurt your—or Elena's—feelings."

Sabina was quite moved, more than she would have predicted. In a curious way, Rick was a man of scruples and that made her admire him the more.

"Whatever you say, *caro*. I'm sorry we got into this situation but I'll make sure it doesn't happen again. You know, I think I'm falling in love with you, at least it feels like that."

At this point Elena entered the room, carrying a tray with three tall drinks on it. She was totally naked.

Sabina jumped up off the bed and tried to save the situation from any more awkwardness. "Elena, *cara*, we're going to have to take a rain check on your hospitality, but I just remembered something—we forgot to get our blood tests. And we've got to do it today because the banns are going to be posted tomorrow. I'm so sorry, but we really have to run." While she was blurting this out she was stumbling around the small bedroom gathering up clothes, hers and Rick's, tossing him his while trying to get into hers any which way.

Elena, totally baffled now, tried to put a good face on things. She picked up a drink, and offering the tray to the other two, she said, "Well at least, let me offer a toast to the happy couple. May you have a long life together filled with happiness."

They clinked glasses and sipped their drinks. Elena went to get herself a robe from the next room.

Ciaccio was restlessly pacing back and forth. He had never been good at waiting and here he was waiting for Rick to return. It was late in the evening. Every couple of minutes he'd look at his watch. It was getting close to midnight.

He finally had to stop calling Sabina's house—the maid began to sound exasperated with his calls. Finally, she simply took the phone off the hook.

Ciaccio's mind was awhirl with terrible thoughts. There had been some terrible auto accident. Maybe some terrorist had kidnapped Rick and Sabina. Or the Red Brigades. Worst of all— Rick had changed his mind again and had flown back to California. Ciaccio was at the end of his tether. So far, he had kept a lid on his feelings and thoughts by discreetly sniffing a little coke throughout the evening. But even coke has its limits as a pacifier. Ciaccio was numb at this point, but far from tranquil. He remembered a drug that was sitting in his medicine cabinet—a friend had given it to him as a present some months ago. Poppers, technically knows as amyl nitrite. The friend had said, "It's not really a drug. You can get them without a prescription at any drugstore. It has one great virtue—it prolongs and intensifies the effects of coke."

Now was the time to see if his friend was bullshitting him or not. He searched the medicine cabinet and found the small bottle. He unscrewed the top and sniffed deeply from the top of the bottle—it was filled with a colorless liquid. The smell was offputting and sort of rancid, but the effect was as described. All at once, he felt so calm, so light-headed and ethereal he was positively floating. His thoughts were calm and serene.

He took the bottle back into the vestibule where he had been pacing. He took another sniff. He was still concerned about Rick, but the terrible anguish was gone.

The thing Ciaccio hated about the hours he'd spent worrying was that it underlined to him how totally he was in Rick's thrall. Without Rick he ceased to exist.

Finally, he heard the elevator coming up. He sat down, trying to seem nonchalant—he took one last sniff of the poppers. He pulled his silk robe about himself and crossed his legs, looking for all the world like a man perfectly at peace with himself and the universe.

161

The door opened. Rick appeared looking radiant as usual.

Ciaccio got up and went to him. Suddenly he lost his cool. "Where have you been? Do you know what time it is? I was worried sick!"

Ever so casually, Rick said, "I'm sorry. We drove out to Brianza to a friend of Sabina's. One thing led to another. She insisted we stay for dinner. You know how these things happen."

"You could have called."

"I tried several times. The phone was always busy."

"You know I have several lines. One of them would have gotten through. You're lying." He reached out and slapped Rick on the cheek. Rick's reaction was not long in coming. He punched Ciaccio in the shoulder and Ciaccio suddenly found himself sprawled on the floor at Rick's feet.

"Don't you ever lift your hand to me like that again. Not ever," Rick hissed, his face red with feeling.

Ciaccio looked up at Rick from his place on the floor and started crying, "Oh Rick, I'm so sorry. I didn't think."

Rick held out his hand to help Ciaccio up onto his feet. "And I'm sorry I hit you."

As Ciaccio was being helped up he stared at that powerful arm that had so easily decked him. All of a sudden he realized he was turned on in a new way.

As he stood up, he whispered, "Hit me. Hit me again."

Rick just shook his head. "Forget it. It's late, let's go to bed."

"No, please, Rick, just once. Hit me again." Ciaccio threw off his robe to reveal himself naked. He bent over the armchair offering Rick his butt. "I mean it. Use your belt."

"You're sure?"

"I beg you."

Everything was turning out fine. Rick had been quite worried about returning so late and Ciaccio's nagging him about being left alone for so long. Now there was this new, totally unexpected development.

With a slow, tantalizingly measured movement, Rick

removed his Gucci belt and folded it in half.

Ciaccio had returned to the floor. Now he was lying spread-eagled on it.

"Are you ready?"

"Yes, beat me," Ciaccio whispered, writhing about, his rock hard cock rubbing against the carpeting. "Anywhere where it won't show."

"It will be our little secret," Rick said. He swung the belt. He hit Ciaccio on the back. The sound was quite satisfyingly loud, but it left no mark. That was fine by Rick. He had no desire to turn this game into an exercise of cruelty. Even though Ciaccio kept yelling "Harder, harder!" Rick persisted in hitting him gently. However, the novelty of the situation was getting to him and he felt himself getting turned on.

After the extraordinary session earlier with Sabina, Rick was concerned that he would not be able to satisfy Ciaccio on his return. But no, with each stroke he could feel desire rising up in him.

Finally, Ciaccio gasped, "That's enough."

"Did I hurt you?" Rick asked as he put away the belt.

"It was so wonderful," Ciaccio said as he stood, his hardon rigidly sticking out.

Rick swept him up in his arms. Ciaccio was completely wiped out from a combination of coke and poppers before Rick's return and the added fillip of the beating as well.

"Carry me to bed, *caro*," Ciaccio murmured into Rick's chest.

Rick thought, between the brother and the sister, I'm going to be worn to a frazzle in no time if I don't take care of myself.

Chapter 17

*G*iovanna was sometimes scared, much more often anxious. It was the anxiety that was getting to her. Anxiety is, after all, nothing more than a nameless fear, and what can't be named is that much more scary in the long run. For several days now, there had been too much money floating around. She found the huge pile of unpaid bills practically gone, from the most ancient to the most recent. How did Ugo pay all those bills? He had even redeemed the gold necklace and ring her mother had given her when she left home. She never thought she would see the jewelry again. It was that kind of thing that was causing unnamed fears to scurry through her mind. She had a thousand unanswered questions she had no courage to ask. What she didn't have was peace of mind.

Why had Varanni insisted on her setting up the meeting with Jennie Moore (a.k.a. Sarah)? And what was in that ominous package she was supposed to "forget" in Jenny's car?

She made a feeble effort to ask him these questions, but to no avail. All it did was put him into a towering rage—he even threatened to beat her up. So she docilely went along with the scheme. She obeyed him not only out of naked fear; she really loved the guy, he was her whole life. She could even put up with his gambling if she had to.

So, with the same inner strength, the same powerful inner resources she had so often marshalled in the past to deal with the awful debts and the more awful creditors, she dealt as best she could with her fears and anxieties.

It was the height of the dog days, the air was so thick and full of mugginess it was a wonder how anyone was able to breathe it in. The city had a deserted look—any and everybody who could had fled the city for the countryside or the seashore.

Sitting in a nondescript greasy spoon on the edge of town, Giovanna felt herself on the verge of tears.

She looked at her watch—it was two minutes to five. Five was the agreed-upon time for her meeting with Jenny.

There was a car horn. Giovanna looked up—there was Jenny. Behind the wheel of her Dyane, she was like all the Americans, punctual to within a minute. How do they do it, she wondered?

Giovanna watched Jenny as she parked and strolled over to her. Jenny was as beautiful as she was punctual. She was doing O.K. financially too, if the car was any indication. She wondered if Jenny would revert to type like all the other Barbies—after her time in the sun in the fashion industry—always assuming she wasn't done in by drugs or some such obstacle—she would return to her hometown and marry her high school sweetheart and settle into a bland and uneventful domestic life as a housewife.

Smelling of lily-of-the-valley, Jenny sat down.

"Giovanna,! You're looking good. It's been awhile. How have you been?"

"Pretty good. And you?"

"Aside from the fact I have to stay in Milan because of work—how I long to be swimming in the sea right now—I'm doing great."

"How about a drink?"

"I'll skip it. It only makes me sweat more and I don't need that."

The amenities over with, they fell into an uncomfortable silence.

Jenny broke it by saying, "I was quite surprised to get your call. Those two weeks I spent with your agency and that pig Varanni certainly weren't filled with joy and happiness."

"I'm sorry about that, Jenny."

"Call me Sarah. That's my name now. More stylish, don't you think?"

"Let me get down to business then. Varanni is reorganizing the agency from top to bottom and he'd like to hook up again with some of his former models."

Jenny was outraged. "If you think I'd go back and work for the Image Agency, you must be out of your mind. It's the pits."

Even Giovanna had to smile at this. "Now we know we're not in the top ten. No, I didn't make my point clearly. You're in a totally different category now. But, if you know of any models who are just starting out . . . "

"And you want me to steer them toward the Image Agency! I am truly amazed at your gall. I'm sorry, Giovanna, I'm sure this has nothing to do with you, it's all Varanni's idea. What a lowlife he is!"

All of Giovanna's protective instincts rose to the fore. O.K. she realized the Image Agency wasn't the creme de la creme, but Jenny's total scorn was uncalled for. Especially what she said about Varanni.

Repressing her anger and her tears, Giovanna kept up a cheery front. Smiling, she asked, "Well then. What should I tell Ugo?"

"Tell him to go fuck himself."

"That's not a very nice message to pass along."

"Listen, Giovanna, your call aroused my curiosity. And I don't

167

mind seeing you again. I like you, I think you're simpática. But take my advice. Drop that creep. He'll only drag you down. I could help you try and get work somewhere else, someplace reputable."

Jenny got up. "I've got to go."

Giovanna stood too. "You're leaving?"

"What's there left to say? We've both had our say. Besides I've got another appointment."

"Which way are you going?"

"Downtown. Need a lift?"

"Not far. The nearest subway station will be fine."

"Sure, no problem. Come on."

Jenny drove without speaking. Using a loose buckle on her shoe as a ruse, Giovanna took the package out of her pocket and slipped it under the seat. After all that Jenny had said, if it turned out the package held a bomb, Giovanna wouldn't mind.

When she got out of the car at the subway station she noticed Varanni in an anonymous-looking 127 not far behind.

"Thanks for the lift," she said and slammed the door so hard the entire car shook.

Jenny pulled away into traffic.

Varanni nudged Lo Porro, who was sitting next to him in the 127.

"That's the car, the Dyane," he said, as Giovanna disappeared into the entrance to the subway. "And that's the one we're after, driving."

"Are you sure the stuff's been planted?"

"Completely. We'd worked it out. If anything had gone wrong, Giovanna would have headed toward the other direction, into the park."

"All dirty tricks look alike."

"Are you getting philosophical or are you going to lecture me? Either way, I'd rather be spared your thoughts."

"What good would it do anyhow? A guy like you, with your gutter mentality, would never understand anyhow. I still think it's

168

a dirty trick."

"O.K. Now here's where you come in. When are you going to spring into action?"

"Tonight. And after tonight, we're through. You can't use me any more. That's final."

"Don't worry. After tonight we're even. Now get out. Your feet are stinking up the car."

"Lo Porro predicts, you're going to wind up someday at the bottom of the river," he said as he got out of the 127. "That day I will take off from work and celebrate."

Jenny didn't really have an appointment. She had said that so she wouldn't have to drive Giovanna home and run the risk of bumping into Varanni. The very thought of him gave her the ooglie-wooglies.

Soon after she had first arrived in Milan, Varanni had finagled and tricked her into his bed and she still felt a sense of disgust whenever she thought about the encounter. He was a walking definition of deadbeat, something that flourishes on the margin of society, living off it. Thinking of him gave her a feeling of menace. She couldn't justify the feeling with words, it was pure instinct. But she trusted her instincts.

Jenny drove to the Piazza San Babila. Here she was in the most elegant square in all Italy and everything was closed—the shops, the cafes, the theaters. If she hadn't known that in Bel Reame, in air-conditioned workshops there was a small army of people working away on the new fall collections, she would have thought there had been an air raid and Milan had been totally deserted by its citizenry.

Her meeting with Giovanna had made her nervous and edgy. She had agreed to the meeting, hoping Giovanna had called on her own initiative. Not a chance. She was still Varanni's puppet.

There was no sign of life in the square, not even a stray cat. She decided to return home. As she was making a U turn, a middle-aged man turned up in front of her car, appearing from nowhere, it seemed. He also seemed vaguely familiar.

He was in search of a cab. Jenny recognized him by his icy blue eyes. Sam Violante, a New Yorker. She had met him at a party at Diovisi's a season or two ago. She remembered he struck her as very wealthy—he wore a lot of jewelry for a man. He also wore the best suit money could buy. And the best silk shirt under it.

They had danced together for a bit that night. She was charmed by him. He seemed to be courting her, in a most gentlemanly fashion. There was nothing self-important or aggressive about him, unlike the young guys she dated. Jenny preferred middle-aged men—they had more tact, more savoir faire. It wasn't that men were such an overwhelming consideration in Jenny's life, but when she thought about it, she realized her preference for older men was real.

After that evening, she hadn't thought about Violante further. Her thoughts were more general than specific on the subject. Now—instinctively—she got out of the car and walked over to him, smiling.

"Good evening, Mr. Violante."

"Jenny! How are you doing?" he replied, shaking her hand. "I gave my chauffeur the day off. I decided to go to the lakes but now I can't find a cab for the life of me. The city is deserted."

"I could drive you," she said impulsively, motioning toward her car.

She was flattered that not only did he recognize her, he remembered her name.

Violante smiled. "That would be great. But I'm sure I'm imposing, you must have things to do."

Getting into the car she said, "Is that your genteel way of asking if I'm seeing anyone? The answer's no."

"I wouldn't think of inquiring into your private life like that," he said, getting in on his side.

"Keep the window closed, there's air conditioning, Mr. Violante."

"Come on now. You've got to call me Sam."

170

Jenny felt swell now. All the earlier unease, the queasiness of the meeting with Giovanna was gone. She was glad to drive Sam out to the lakes—with him at her side she felt wrapped in a sense of security, she felt protected.

She had heard some rumors about him. The word was that he had something to do, in a rather major way, with racketeering. That didn't faze Jenny. The story she'd heard was that Violante, in exchange for control of the American market for Diovisi, used the fashion house for money-laundering purposes. One dollar washed the other. Jenny stuck to her instincts and they told her Violante was a good man.

Looking at her as she drove, he said, "A penny for your thoughts."

"I'm thinking about you, truth to tell."

"Do you find me very boring?"

Vehemently Jenny turned to him and said, "How can you say that. On the contrary," her eyes returned to the road—"I like you. I think you're handsome and you give me a sense of protection."

"Do you know how old I am?"

"Not really, I can guess—late forties?"

"I'm fifty-two. Thirty-one years older than you."

Jenny was dumbstruck. Not at the fact he was fifty-two, but that somehow—he must have made some inquiries—he knew *her* age.

"How do you know my age?"

"It wasn't hard to find out. That night at the villa when we danced together I took a shine to you. So I asked a few questions and got a few answers."

Jenny smiled. "What you're saying is you're interested in me."

"I was. I mean, I am. What I mean is, after that night I got cold feet. I thought a woman as young and vibrant as you couldn't get serious over an old fart like me. You need to go out and dance, travel, have fun, make love six times a day—"

"At least!" She slammed on the brakes and pulled the car over to the side of the road.

"How can you think such thoughts! And not consult me about the matter." She was all worked up. "I'm different in a lot of ways from the other models. For one thing, a man your age is a turn-on for me. I like mature people, not kids."

"What if people were to tell you I'm mixed up with some shady business deals?"

"Idle gossip. I don't pay attention to that kind of nonsense."

"What if it turned out I really was some kind of gangster?"

"You can't put me off with that. I bet it's a lot more interesting than being, say, an accountant."

He turned to her and said, "Turn this crate around, Jenny. We're going back to Milan."

Jenny's face fell. "So this is the end of our brief romance?"

"Just the opposite. I was supposed to go to New York in a couple of days—unavoidable business. Now I'm going to go tomorrow, tonight if I can still get a flight. When I come back—my business won't take more than a couple of days—we can pick up the pieces and start putting it all together. We could go away for a long vacation."

"I can't. The fall fashion show. There's the try-ons and all the rest."

"If you want, I'll speak to Lorenzo—get him to release you from your contract."

"But I don't want to get out of my contract. I've made all these plans and I want to follow through on them."

"What kind of plans, may I ask?"

"Saving a nest egg for my retirement, for one. Models retire very early on in life. I'm determined to save two hundred thousand dollars at the very least."

"I like an independent woman. How close are you to your goal?"

"Not all that far away, actually."

"What if I were to . . . "

"No! I feel very strongly about this. It's something I have to do for myself. I don't want you to subsidize me. Besides, I enjoy

172

my work."

"It's settled. When I return, we'll vacation right here in Milan. The important thing is that we'll be together."

Jenny threw her arms around Sam and gave him a big hug and a kiss. She switched on the ignition and turned the car around, heading back for Milan.

Driving back, Jenny felt enormously happy. Again she was leaning heavily on her instincts, but they hadn't steered her wrong yet. She felt she'd met the man she'd been looking for all along, albeit unconsciously. A strong, mature, yet gentle man, who knew what he wanted out of life. Her definition of a real man.

"Where shall I drop you?" she asked as they reentered the city.

"I'm staying at the Imperiale. I'll have to pack."

"Can I hang around, maybe drive you to the airport later?"

"No, you go home."

"When will you get back?"

"The far outside—three days at the most."

Jenny had a slew of questions to ask. She needed him to comfort her, to reassure her, to talk of this dream they had created together. Not now. This wasn't the right time.

Anyhow, she had a feeling words were almost useless with a man like Sam Violante. Everything about him would lead one to think he was a man of few words and decisive actions. He was so strong, so secure.

"I'll be waiting," she said as he got out of the car.

"Think of me tonight. And the nights until I return."

He gave her a wink. She blew him a kiss on her fingertips. An old, romantic gesture. Something only a mature man would appreciate.

Lo Porro was lying in wait. He'd cadged a police car through some finagling. In the car with him was Rosario Napoli, a young rookie who was born crooked. Lo Porro had enough on him to get him suspended. He would be good for this mission. He knew something shady was going on, but he had enough smarts to ask a bare minimum of questions. There was a young foreign woman who needed to be taught a little lesson—nothing extreme. Just scare her a little.

They sat there like statues in the police car in front of her home, waiting, waiting.

Lo Porro knew what to do. He'd worked out all the details in advance. As soon as they picked her up, Lo Porro would call Varanni. They'd take her to police headquarters, entering the back way—it was always unstaffed by night. She'd think she was in serious trouble.

Varanni would show up then, ready to help her out of her unpleasant fix. In exchange for getting her out of a jam, of course he might expect a favor or two in return, out of gratitude on her part, if nothing else.

What was taking this Jenny Moore (a.k.a. Sarah) so long? Where was she anyhow? Waiting like this made both of them nervous as cats.

"Do we have to wait much longer?" Rosario asked.

"We'll wait as long as we have to."

"What's she look like? Is she sexy?"

"From the description she could drive a poor man blind. But this isn't a usual case, Rosario. We can't lay a finger on her, understand?"

"Too bad. Can't you tell me anything more about this operation?"

"Politics, buddy. It all comes down to politics. It's all above our heads. Don't even try to understand."

Lo Porro spotted the Dyane pulling up. He switched on the engine and burned rubber cutting Jenny off with his vehicle.

Jenny looked up in surprise. She was so lost in her own thoughts they could have dropped from the sky for all she knew.

Lo Porro said, trying to sound as official as possible, "Your papers, please."

"What have I done wrong, officer?"

Lo Porro flashed his card and repeated in a sterner voice than

174

before, "Your papers."

"They're in the glove compartment," she said.

She was reaching for them when he stopped her. "I'll get them," he said.

"You act as if I might have a gun in there."

"Don't be cute. And don't try anything funny. My partner's got you covered."

"Are you for real?"

Lo Porro moved decisively. He reached under the passenger seat and removed a box. He opened it gingerly. In the light of the street lamp it gave off an eerie glow. White, finely ground powder. Jenny recognized it instantly as cocaine. She was stunned.

"You're in trouble, miss. Come along with us."

"I've never seen that before."

"We've heard that line before. You'll have to come to the station house with us."

Her thoughts still on Sam, she asked, "Will it take long?"

Lo Porro tried to sound his most menacing when he answered. "There's no way of knowing."

Chapter 18

For some reason, it's much easier to see other people's self-destructive behavior than one's own. Diana Rau was miserable over what she perceived as Inna's self-destructive ways. Inna seemed to be literally throwing her life away with abandon. Nature had lavished its gifts on Inna and Inna couldn't care less. What a waste, Diana thought. Inna was right on the brink of establishing herself as an international superstar fashion model, yet she was seemingly impervious to that glorious possibility.

Diana was no moralist striking some stern Calvinistic pose. When she was starting out as a young unknown model in the early days of her career, she slept around plenty. The main difference, as she saw it, was she was canny enough to use sex as a tool to advance her career. Even, in a way, to this day, if one looked at her relationship with Kao in the proper light. No, Diana was dismayed at Inna's rampant sexing around because it seemed to stem from a desire to have a constant itch constantly scratched. She was not whoring around *intelligently*.

Diana didn't give much credence, either, to psychologically oriented theories about nymphomania etc. She looked upon Inna's activity the way she would a chocoholic being locked up in a candy factory.

Diana had plans for Inna, big plans. She felt Inna would be the ideal model to represent her line when it was ready for the public. In the name of business, then, Diana saw it as her task to impose some discipline on Inna and make her straighten up and fly right.

Her game plan went something like this: She meant to start Diana Rau Fashions as an exclusive house, affordable by only the fabulously wealthy. Then, after it was established as the height of chic, would she expand into the large mass world markets— here Kao's connections would be invaluable. And the face to launch this mighty ship would be Inna's.

Fuxia Taylor was dead. She had died instantly and gruesomely in a car accident. Her car had hit a divider, turned over several times and finally crashed into a tree, but not before Fuxia's gorgeous head had been severed from her gorgeous body. The coroner had estimated she must have been going at least 90 miles an hour to create the impact she did. The autopsy report on the kinds and amounts of drugs in her system read like a catalogue of controlled substances.

Diana hoped the news of Fuxia's death would have a sobering effect on Inna. She needed Inna. All her years paying her dues in the fashion industry and now she was so close to achieving her grand ambition, it felt within reach. She would not let Inna—or anybody else fuck up her plans.

She then thought of Andrea and a warm trickle of love made her feel momentarily boneless as it spread throughout her whole body. He was her one true vulnerability. Because she had never been truly in love before, she had built up no defenses, no stratagems against its onslaught. She had a vision that horrified

178

her—she could see herself giving up everything—her ambitions, the luxuries and habits of a lifetime—to go off somewhere obscure and live the rest of her days, even in poverty if necessary, with Andrea. What was particularly horrible about this vision was that she saw herself living it and *being happy.*

She forced herself to put the vision and all thoughts of Andrea aside. It was quite a struggle. She gritted her teeth and clenched her hands into fists and forced herself to return to plans for Diana Rau Fashions. She was too close to the finish line. Work must come first.

She would get to work on Inna.

Her eyes glazed and bloodshot from a combination of drugs, sex and lack of sleep, Inna stumbled back into the room after a trip to get something cold to drink from the refrigerator. She couldn't even swallow, her mouth had been so dry.

There were three young men, all asleep and snoring. Fortunately the bed was oversize—it could accommodate a fourth body if it had to, say, for instance, Inna's. They had been at it steadily for a couple of days straight. She had picked them up. Walking along the street, they had driven up and, more out of a feeling of youthful high spirits than rampant sexuality, they had good-naturedly called out a compliment to her. She looked at them and found them all cute and sexy. She walked over to the car and said, "How's about the four of us get together and play?"

Misunderstanding her, thinking her to be a hooker, the one closest to her asked, "How much?"

Making herself clearer to the point, she said, "I'm not after your money. I want your bodies."

One of their most cherished pornographic fantasies seemed to be actually coming true. They gaped at her, not believing such a beautiful, angelically pretty young woman had said what they'd just heard her say. They were all simple guys, all from the same blue-collar neighborhood. They were ideal for Inna's purposes. Their gossip would never reach her world. They leapt at the opportunity and she got in the car and they drove to the modest apartment of the driver—an auto mechanic, it turned out.

As soon as they got to the apartment, Inna took complete charge. She ordered them to strip, even as she was taking her own clothes off. She then ordered them onto the bed where she proceeded to go down on one while she manipulated the cocks of the others with her hands. Then she insisted they fuck her. They obliged, sometimes singly, sometimes in pairs. Throughout it all, she still was able to somehow maintain the look of a young maiden, one that might have sat for the Madonna in some fifteenth-century Virgin and Child painting.

Every so often, when she needed refueling, she went off to the bathroom where she snorted another couple of lines of coke. Inconsiderately, she didn't offer any to her playmates.

Looking at the three sleeping figures she shook her head. She went over to the bed and started poking away at them. "Is this what you think a bed is for—sleeping?"

One of them opened his eyes a crack and said, "We're not made of iron, baby. Give us a break."

"Are you saying you're *tired*?"

"Tired! I'm wiped out!"

"We'll see about that."

Kneeling over the bodies of the other two guys who were blissfully asleep, she leaned over and got the smartass in a liplock. In no time flat, as she knew it would, his cock was quiveringly rigid. She flopped down on the bed and said to him, "Give it to me."

"Where do you want it, baby?"

"Anywhere you want to put it. You decide."

He started fucking her, violently enough to satisfy her and to wake up the other two as well. One of them leaned over and started licking her nipples as he tried to maneuver himself in such a way as to place his cock in her mouth. The third, the auto mechanic, got up and left the bed. He had had enough—more than enough. All he wanted was for everybody to go home so he

180

could get some real sleep.

Spotting Inna's purse, he got an idea. He went and took it into the hallway and started searching through it for some kind of ID.

Kao had wired from India that he would be with her shortly. Andrea was up in his garret, impatiently waiting for her to join him. But Diana couldn't think about either. She was really worried about Inna. She'd checked out all of Inna's hangouts and friends and turned up only one fact—no one had seen Inna for a couple of days.

The phone rang. Diana was so nervous its ring made her jump involuntarily.

"Is this the Delfino home?" It was the voice of a young man.

"No. I mean yes, if you're calling about Inna."

"Are you her mother?"

"In loco parentis. I'm her aunt."

"Can I talk . . . openly?"

"What do you mean? Has something happened to Inna? Is she all right?"

"She's O.K. But here's the problem. She's been in my apartment for close to two days and we can't seem to get rid of her and end the party."

"Who is this 'we'?"

"Me and a couple of friends."

It all came clear to Diana. A smile came to her lips as she thought, Poor guy, Inna's made him cry uncle.

"What do you want from me?" Diana asked a bit cautiously, afraid blackmail might be this guy's motive for calling. When she found out all he wanted her to do was come take Inna home, she heaved a sigh of relief.

"I'll come immediately. What's the address?"

The young man gave her the address and added, "Please hurry," in a tone that sounded positively plaintive.

She hung up and prepared to leave. This was the last straw.

Tonight, no matter what state Inna was in, Diana was going to have it out with her. She would get tough, if she had to. Inna would be made to behave properly, whether she liked it or not.

Before leaving, Diana raced upstairs to Andrea.

He was lying on the bed reading. When she entered, he put his book down, smiled lovingly and held his arms out to her.

"Hi, darling," he said.

"Andrea, I'd love to spend some time with you but I've got to go out. Inna's in trouble."

"Anything serious?"

"In a sense, no. She's not being held by the police or anything like that. I'll tell you all about it when I get back."

"It's only my opinion, but she sounds like more trouble than she's worth."

"She's my niece, after all. I'm her guardian. And I care about what happens to her. She reminds me a lot of myself when I was her age."

"Were you that mixed up?"

"It was a different time—drugs weren't so omnipresent as they now are."

"You don't have to apologize for your past, *cara*, especially to me. It's your present and future I'm interested in."

"Let me go. The sooner I go the sooner I'll get back."

"Will we have time to be together later?"

"Yes, but it'll be quite late, not until I have it out with Inna and get her off to bed."

A few minutes later, wearing dark glasses and a kerchief so she wouldn't be recognized, Diana drove toward the working-class neighborhood where her phone caller lived. The streets were mostly deserted, a few people milling about among the melon stalls. Ordinary people doing mundane things. With Andrea, she could be content with such an unglamorous existence.

Turning into the street of the address she spotted a good-looking young man leaning against the entrance to the building. She got out of the car and walked over to him.

"I'm Inna's aunt. Were you the one I spoke to on the phone?"

"Yes."

"Where's Inna?"

"Upstairs. With my friends."

"I'm curious. Why did you call me?"

"Get rid of her."

"You're three men and you couldn't get rid of one woman?"

"We'd never met anybody like her before. Even a train stops sometimes. But not her. When I opened her purse to get your number, I found some coke. Me and my buddies don't want any trouble."

"You're right. Can we go up now?"

"Follow me."

Even though she knew pretty accurately what she would see when she entered the bedroom, Diana found herself surprisingly upset at the spectacle on the bed. She realized how much she really loved Inna, and felt the need to protect her, if necessary, from her own self-destructive impulses.

She walked over to the bed. "We have to go now, Inna," she said.

One of the guys looked up at her and said, "Who the fuck are you?"

The auto mechanic spoke up then. "She's her aunt. I called her to come take her niece home. Party's over."

Not all that reluctantly, the two guys on the bed got up and trudged off to the bathroom. The third one tactfully withdrew into the other room.

Picking up Inna's clothes which had been lying in a jumble on the floor, Diana said, "Come on, Inna. It's late."

"Late for what?"

"Late, period."

"You know, Diana, you are a royal pain in the ass. Get off my back. Why'd you have to come and break up the party, sticking your nose where it doesn't belong?"

Diana slapped Inna's cheek hard.

"You'll pay for that, bitch. Just wait and see," Inna said.

"You're coming with me. I don't want to see you ending up like Fuxia Taylor."

Puzzled, Inna asked, "What's Fuxia got to do with all this?"

"I'm sorry. I thought you knew. Fuxia stole a car and, stoned and drunk, crashed the thing to smithereens. Fuxia's dead, Inna."

Inna seemed to be coming out of a stupor. She slowly grasped what Diana had just said. Tears came to her eyes involuntarily.

"Is that true, Diana?"

"I'm sorry to say it is. They found a letter—it was for you. A love letter."

Inna broke down. Crying piteously, she said, "It's all my fault. I killed her."

"Come, *cara*. Let's go home."

On the ride back, Inna started searching through her purse. "If you're looking for the coke, forget it. I flushed it away back there. Your coke days are over for now."

Inna fell into a brooding silence and stayed that way the rest of the way home.

While Inna was showering, Diana made some camomile tea. It was soothing and restorative. Her own mother used to make it for her when she was a little girl and needed to be calmed down when she was upset.

She would use Fuxia's stupid and pointless death as a cautionary tale for Inna. Follow in that pathway, and it would be inevitable to wind up in a prematurely early grave. She hoped she could get through to Inna.

The phone rang. It was Kao, calling from the Milan airport. He would take a cab and join her within the hour.

Diana had been caught off guard by Kao's call. She should have told him to go to a hotel, that she'd speak to him tomorrow. What with the confusion and turmoil she'd just gone through with Inna, she'd agreed to his coming over without thinking.

She felt a bit like the philandering husband in a French farce.

Kao was coming over. So, instead of the long heart-to-heart she meant to have with Inna, she sent her off to bed. Fortunately, without the coke to shore her up, Inna was in a very subdued mood and put up no argument.

Then Diana ran upstairs to Andrea, heading him off at the pass, so to speak. Nothing had changed. She found him lying in bed, still reading.

"Finally. I thought you'd never get here," he said, putting down his book.

"I can't spend time with you tonight, I'm sorry."

In an understanding tone of voice, he said, "Is Inna being that difficult?"

"Inna's already in bed."

"Then what's the problem?"

"Kao just called from the airport. He'll be here soon."

"And Kao takes priority over me, I suppose."

"Oh, Andrea, please don't be difficult. Try and understand. He's my partner, my major backer."

"And your lover."

"He did bring up the possibility of a marriage sometime in the future."

"Where does all this leave me? Am I some kind of toy, something you play with now and then when you have a spare moment and then put back in the closet?"

"We've already discussed this. I was hoping you'd understand."

"I certainly do understand. You say you love me, meanwhile you're engaged to—and making love with—another man."

Diana felt totally helpless, defeated.

"I told you, it's strictly a business arrangement on my part. For the most part, Kao feels the same way."

"That's it!" He jumped out of bed and started getting dressed.

"What are you doing?"

"I've had it. I'm tired of being the fifth wheel around here."

Diana ran over to him and clutched at his back. "Please don't go away. Stay, I beg you."

He shook her off like some annoying spaniel wanting attention. "Don't even try to stop me. You won't succeed."

"But where will you go?"

"That doesn't concern you any longer."

"Will you come back?"

"Let me know when you're willing to be seen with me in public."

He gave her a harsh shove, pushing her aside, and stormed out the door. Diana collapsed in uncontrollable sobs on the bed. The sheets were permeated with Andrea's special smell.

She had no time to indulge herself in tears. Kao was ringing the doorbell. She let him in and asked him to wait in the living room. She ran into the bathroom and proceeded to splash cold water onto her eyes to bring down the swelling.

By the time she came back out, one would never know she'd been under any kind of stress earlier that day. She was made up, and gave off a radiant glow. She had revivified herself with some coke as well as the cold water. To think such a short while before she had flushed away all of Inna's coke . . . But there was a world of difference between them, as Diana saw it. Inna was abusing the drug. Diana was using it judiciously for business purposes. A world of difference.

"I've rarely seen you looking better," Kao said.

"How kind of you to say that," she said as she sat down opposite him on the couch.

Chapter 19

*J*enny fought valiantly to hold back the tears. She'd have to be strong. Even though she felt as if she were standing on the edge of an abyss, she vowed she would hold on to her cool. She mustn't let them get to her in that way. One thing was certain—the coke had been found in her car. She hadn't the vaguest idea how it got there, but they didn't believe that for a minute.

For the moment, they had left her alone in this bare and cheerless room. She didn't mind the young cop so much, but the older one gave her the creeps. Didn't he ever bathe? He smelled like a goat in heat.

She was in a jam and she knew it. The last thing she needed was a run in with the police—on a drug charge, no less. The least of it would be losing all the leverage she'd made in the modeling business. There was the possibility of jail—or, in some sense even worse, deportation. In any event, her career would be shot. Her past was rising up to haunt her. Although now she was in complete control of her life, when she'd first arrived in Italy she had gone completely wild—not so much emphasis on the sex, but at one point she certainly had a rep among the heavier drug users. When she'd lived at the Princess Clithilde, she snorted with the best of them. Although that was so long ago it seemed part of another life, it could rise up now and put the finishing touches on her career.

Her thoughts shifted to Sam Violante. Whatever else, she mustn't involve him in all this. Maybe the cops had been trailing her for a long time. If that was the case, two strong possibilities came to mind. It couldn't be Violante they were after, since she had met him again by the purest of accidents. Of course, he might have inadvertently put the package in her car *because* she was so safe. If that were the case, she'd have to clam up to protect him. The other possibility was that—for some reason totally unknown to her—the coke had been planted in her car by the police themselves. Why, she had no idea.

A sad smile stole over her face as she thought of Sam Violante. She couldn't have planned meeting him the way she did in the Piazza San Babila, but in retrospect the meeting had seemed almost predestined. Inadvertently she had connected with the kind of man she dreamed of, a strong, caring man who would offer her a sense of protection and solace. Perhaps it was an appointment in Samarra—fated to be.

Just then, the cop who stank returned to the room. A smile closer to a smirk played across his lips.

"You could make things a lot easier for all of us if you'd come clean and confess," he said.

"I want a lawyer. I'm not saying anything until I get a lawyer," Jenny replied.

He shook his head. "Can't you get it through your head, once and for all, this isn't America. Those kinds of rights don't exist here."

"Then leave me alone. I have nothing further to say."

The cop got to his feet. She was terrified he would hit her.

In the small, close room, his smell was so overpowering she felt on the verge of gagging.

"Let's face the facts. There's no avoiding the central one—we found the package of coke in your car. That's possession, right there."

"I want a lawyer."

"O.K. Maybe you didn't own the stuff—you were keeping it for a friend who left it in your car. That's possible."

Jenny came to stiff attention. Was that last statement of the cop's meant to hint in the direction of Sam's involvement?

She weighed all the pros and cons in her mind. The end result was that she decided she'd rather ruin her modeling career than jeopardize Violante in any way. Was she crazy? Was she really infatuated with him that much?

"O.K.," she said. "I'm ready to confess."

The cop fell openmouthed in astonishment. He hadn't expected this development. "Confess what?" he asked.

"The drug. I bought it from a stranger. I don't know his name. It was for my own personal use."

The cop stood there, his mouth hanging open. "This is your confession?"

"Isn't it what you were after?"

Abruptly changing the subject, he said, "We've searched your apartment. We went through your Rolodex. We found a friend of yours who's willing to vouch for you."

Jenny was terrified by a new thought. If the friend he was referring to turned out to be Diovisi, the game was over. He'd come to her rescue, sure, go bail for her, no doubt about that. But instantly she would be stricken from his list, and from all the other reputable lists in town. More than once, Diovisi had talked about this very subject. "Do whatever you want," he'd say. "Fuck who you want, drink all you want, snort all you want. But don't get caught doing so. Discretion is the name of the game. If the word gets out, you're through in this business. Do whatever you want, but don't let it reflect on your work."

She clung to the hope that the friend he referred to wasn't Diovisi.

"Did you contact this friend?"

"Sure did," Lo Porro said. "By sheer coincidence, he happens to be an old acquaintance of mine, so I know for a fact what a trustworthy gentleman he is."

"Who is it?"

"You'll find out soon enough. He showed immense concern for your plight and said he would get here as soon as he could."

Jenny's heart did a couple of flipflops. That moment, the young cop was escorting Ugo Varanni into the room. *That* was the trustworthy gentleman! But in her present circumstances, even Varanni looked good to her, anybody who promised to get her out of that room.

"Hi, Jenny," Varanni said as he pulled up a chair.

"You're just in time," she said.

"Officer Lo Porro here is an old friend of mine. I know he's concerned about you. He has a daughter just your age."

"I'm sure his daughter is very nice. What will it cost to get me out of here?"

"Forget it, I've already taken care of all the formalities. You're free to go."

"I suppose you want something from me, some return of the favor."

"I always said you're no dummy. You know me well enough to know I never do something for the pleasure of making the world a better place. Now as I recall, just a few hours ago, for instance, you said some unfriendly things about me."

"We've never been friends, you know that."

"But now you need me."

"Cut the crap. What is it you want from me?"

Jenny was ready to do whatever it was Varanni asked if it meant erasing this entire episode from the official record—if it meant that Sam Violante wouldn't be affected in any way. She hoped and prayed as hard as she could that Varanni's condition was not that she go to bed with him, for she knew, no matter how truly disgusting the prospect, she would do it.

Varanni nodded to the cops, who left silently.

"I repeat, what is it you want from me?" Oh, please, she thought, not sex.

"If you want to get out of this mess, wipe it off the police blotter entirely, you'll have to give me something in exchange."

"Fine, I understand that. What?"

Varanni reached into his pants pocket and pulled out a minuscule camera, tiny, but state of the art.

"You know what this is?"

"It's a camera. It must have set you back a pretty penny."

"It's yours, a present. Here," he said as he handed it over.

She took it from him warily. "Why are you so generous?"

"I want you to use it to photograph all the designs of Diovisi's new collection. And you've got to do it in the next couple of days."

"That won't be so easy."

"It won't be so difficult either. You have total access to his workrooms. The camera's so small you could hide it, if you had to, in a pack of cigarettes."

"What if I refuse?"

"You will either wind up in jail or be thrown out of Italy. Not to mention what that would do for your love life."

Jenny shivered. There was no way Varanni could know about Sam Violante, and yet he had touched on her most vulnerable point.

"Nothing you mentioned sounds overly appealing. But I want the package of coke back."

Varanni looked at her. What did she want with the coke?

"Don't worry. I'll take the pictures for you."

Varanni went and tapped on the door. The two cops instantly reappeared. "Everything's worked out fine. The lady would like her package back also."

"Of course," Lo Porro said and handed it over to Jenny. "I'm curious," he said. "What do you want it back for? Are you into

191

coke or do you mean to resell it?" He had been hoping, somewhat unreasonably, to get his nostrils on some of the stuff himself.

"I want to make sure this evidence is taken care of properly. Is there a flush toilet around here?"

"I'll take you," Lo Porro said, a pained expression on his face. Such a waste, he thought.

In the toilet, which smelled quite a lot like Lo Porro, Jenny poured the powder into the toilet bowl and flushed. There were still the photographs to be taken.

Two days later, looking terribly nervous, if not positively distraught, Jenny turned up at Varanni's office and slammed two rolls of film down on his desk.

Varanni looked up and smiled. "All done?"

"I'm sorry to say you were absolutely right. It was a piece of cake. Foolish Diovisi, for trusting us all so implicitly."

"Listen if it turns out you're pulling some kind of fast one . . ."

"Keep your shirt on. I photographed the entire collection— the sketches, that is. They're not ready for the models yet."

Varanni stood up and came over to her. "I'm not a vengeful man, Jenny—excuse me, Sarah. Let's let bygones be bygones. Ask me, is there anything I can do for you?"

"There is one thing."

"What?"

"I want you to give me your word, whatever that's worth, never to speak to me again. Not if I was drowning in shit and you had the only lifesaver in town."

"Why do you talk like that? I could be your best friend."

"Friend! Don't make me puke." She whirled around and strode out of the office.

The second she left, Varanni grabbed up the rolls of film and stuffed them into his pants pocket. His problems were over. From here on in, life would be *la dolce vita.*

Varanni came home to a sulky Giovanna. He gave her an

unexpectedly tender caress.

"We're celebrating tonight."

"Celebrating what?"

"Our good luck. Finally the goddess of fortune has decided to smile on us."

Referring to Jenny, for somehow she intuited this all stemmed from the incident with the package, she asked, "What did you do to that girl?"

"Jenny? Nothing, nothing at all. I did her a small favor and she returned the favor. That simple."

"I have a feeling that somehow it wasn't all that simple."

Varanni stopped caressing her. "Will you get off my case?"

Trembling, Giovanna threw her arms around Varanni's shoulders. "For some reason—I can't put it into words—I'm scared, Ugo. Really scared. Nothing good will come of all this."

"Since when did you become a prophet? Money will come of all this. Money and respect. Lots of both. A new contract with Irone Fashions, just for starters. As of today, we're a top ten agency. The first thing we'll have to do is move to smart new quarters."

All this meant nothing to Giovanna. "Please, trust me, Ugo. Let's leave, get out of Milan. Start again somewhere else."

Varanni said, "After all the kowtowing, all the humiliation I've had to put up with here, this city is going to get on its knees and kiss my shoes. After all the crap I've had to swallow over the years—I want the sweet smell of success and the sweet taste of retaliation both."

Giovanna sat down, crying quietly into a handkerchief.

"Don't you dare bring me bad luck," he shouted. "You know a woman's tears bring bad luck. Stop that now."

He stomped out, slamming the door after him.

A few minutes later he was in the studio of a friend who he'd worked with over the years. A photographer with certain standards, but the sterling ability to keep his mouth shut at all times. He was developing the photos Jenny had brought.

A cursory glance was more than enough to confirm to Varanni that Jenny had done her work well. And it looked as if the entire collection was there, she hadn't left anything out. Even to an uneducated eye it was apparent the collection was a knockout, full of freshness and imagination. Classy, that was the word.

"Can I use your phone?" Varanni asked the photographer.

"It's over there. You can pay me for the call later."

He dialled. After several rings, Mittaglia came on the line. "Any news?" he asked.

"Nothing but good news. Exactly what you asked for."

"When can I see the stuff?"

"Right away, if you want."

"Fifteen minutes. Our usual place. I'll be in my Saab."

"Bring the cash. Payment on delivery."

Varanni hung up. Elaborately he made a show of leaving a coin for the call next to the phone.

Alvise looked through the photos. He could have shouted for joy. Whatever his private opinion of Varanni, no one could deny he had accomplished what he'd set out to do. It seemed the entire collection had been photographed. He didn't want to know how Varanni had achieved this. All he was sure of was that it was in some scrungy, totally illegal way.

"How many photos are there altogether?" he asked.

"Seventy-two. Two full rolls."

"Congratulations, Varanni. You did a great job."

Varanni beamed with pleasure. Compliments from men like Alvise Mittaglia were the rarest thing in Varanni's life. And Mittaglia was treating him with respect! There was no condescension in his voice.

"Shall we trade envelopes then?" Mittaglia asked. He took the photos in their large manila envelope as he passed a similarly thick but different-size envelope to Varanni.

Varanni put it into his jacket pocket without opening it.

"Aren't you going to count it?" Mittaglia asked.

"I think, between gentlemen, that's unnecessary."

194

"Well, in that case, *ciao*, and thanks again, Varanni." Clearly he was dismissing Varanni from the car. Varanni didn't move.

"There's some unfinished business we haven't discussed yet."

"What's that?"

"When you originally hired me on for this delicate task, money wasn't the only thing we talked about. To be specific, the subject came up of resuming relations between Irone Fashions and Image Agency."

"I haven't forgotten," Mittaglia said. "We'll get in touch for the next show. This one's all cast."

"How can I be sure I can trust you?" Varanni asked.

"You mean, we're no longer gentlemen?"

"Certainly, no doubt about it. But in our hectic business, occasionally promises can be overlooked, even forgotten."

"Just what is it you want?"

"Nothing less than a signed contract from Irone Fashions. It has to be delivered to my office by five this afternoon, at the latest. That is, if you want the negatives."

"You haven't changed at all, Varanni. You still have all your gutter instincts."

"I'm a businessman. I can't afford to have too many scruples. In fact, the reason you chose me to do this little photo session was precisely because you knew you could count on my lack of scruples."

"I'll have the contract for you this afternoon. Instead of your office, we'll meet here. At four sharp."

Varanni smiled broadly. "It's a pleasure doing business with you."

"Likewise, I'm sure." Varanni got out of the car and Alvise pulled away into traffic.

Giovanna looked up as Varanni strode into the office. He was beaming from ear to ear.

"Here it is, in black and white. Irone's signed us up for his next show. Here's the contract," he said, taking it out of his pocket and waving it in the air.

Giovanna glanced at the contract, her facial expression unchanged. "Ugo, please, listen to me. I really don't mean to come on like a wet blanket, and I know how much this means to you, but . . . "

Varanni scowled at her. "Even in the moment of triumph, you're a downer. It's your provincial background—you were born a small-thinking hick and that's how you'll always be. I've had about enough of your sour puss. Either shape up or take your ass out of here."

Startled, she asked, "Are you throwing me out?"

"As the song goes, that all depends on you. You had better change your attitude and fast. For starters, you can start getting all dolled up. We're going out tonight and doing the town."

"In August? Nothing's open. The town's deserted."

"Who's talking about Milan? We're going to Campione and celebrating all night. We'll come back with money stuffed in all our pockets. God, do I feel lucky!"

"You go yourself. I don't like casinos."

"That's exactly what I mean, about your provincialism. You're only good in the kitchen and in bed. You have no sense of living the good life in style."

"If it makes you feel better to insult me, go ahead. I won't take it personally."

"Of course not. God, it's like punching a pillow. All right, I'll go to Campione myself."

That night Giovanna stayed home and Varanni went to Campione. He lost almost half of the money Alvise Mittaglia had paid him that day. He lost at roulette, he lost at blackjack, he lost at chemin de fer.

This time, however, losing didn't get to him the way it had before. He still had plenty of money left and, best of all, the contract with Irone Fashions.

By the time he decided to return to Milan dawn was appearing in the east. Riding back, one of his back tires blew and he nearly skidded off the road into a ravine.

While changing the tire, he thought, The day started out so well, and then about halfway through it turned around and went steadily downhill. Nevertheless, he was able to ignore his bad luck this time with a philosophical shrug. Things will pick up tomorrow, and the day after that, and the day after that.

Chapter 20

The Moor of Venice hated coming to Milan. He had no affection for the city, its climate, or for that matter its people. And Milan was at its unspeakable worst in summer. The hot muggy air settled so completely over the city it was like trying to breathe with a plastic bag over one's head.

It wasn't only Milan, however, that earned his animus. He hated traveling in general. He had the good luck to have been born and to live in Venice, the most beautiful city in the world. No place, not Paris, not Rome, not the French Riviera, was worth leaving Venice for. He had set up his life in such a way as to avoid traveling at all costs. He was inordinately happy with his life in Venice. Doing business with him meant going to him in Venice, never the other way around. He was content to stay home and concentrate on creating new designs and color combinations, amid the quiet domesticity of his happy family life.

Ubaldo Baraldi had telephoned him the night before. The Little Lord, as Baraldi was known in Bel Reame, told him about the meeting. It seemed the police had broken up a ring of Sardinian gangsters, including the infamous Lisca sisters (rumored to be behind one out of every two kidnappings in Italy for the last ten years), and had found in their possession a mammoth file on every leading figure in the Italian fashion industry—their annual incomes, their estimated worth and, most ominous of all, their daily habits (even down to tiny details such as whether they dressed formally for dinner, where their favorite table was at their favorite restaurant, what kind of wine they preferred with chicken). Of course, all their more human failings and weaknesses were in the file as well. It was obvious they had targeted the fashion industry as their next series of depredations.

Up in arms, Bel Reame decided to have a mass meeting to discuss means of reaction to and protection against such a possibility. So Baraldi had called Zaco Ottoboni in his Venetian workshop and invited him to come.

"They're out to get us—you, me, all of Bel Reame," Baraldi said, a slightly hysterical note apparent in his overripe English accent. (He'd once spent a year at Oxford and the accent was now thicker than ever. The rumor was he'd been in Oxford, to be sure—working in the kitchen of a pub, washing dishes.)

"What do you want from me?" Ottoboni asked, hoping the most that would be asked of him would be some sort of financial contribution.

Ubaldi explained about the meeting in Bel Reame and that his presence would be imperative. "They're kidnappers, after all. Professional kidnappers."

Ottoboni laughed. Kidnappers didn't especially scare him. As an adolescent he'd fought in various boxing tournaments, then, when he reached draft age, he fought in the final days of World War II. He had had an adventurous life after that, seeing various kinds of action in Indochina and Algeria. In fact, he had come to the fashion world by accident. His wife, a former ballerina, had bought a loom and wove sweaters of no special distinction, hoping to sell them through department store chains of the more modest variety. She was notably unsuccessful. One day, for the hell of it, Zaco sat down at the loom, and in no time flat their fortunes started to rise perceptibly.

Ubaldi asked, "What's so funny?" He was very nearly beside himself.

Fearlessly, Ottoboni answered, "I don't see what's so bad about a kidnapping. It would be great publicity, for one thing."

"You don't know how ferocious these Sardinians can get. They're the ones who send the hostage back to the police in installments, first an ear, then a hand. If it weren't so serious I wouldn't be asking you to come. We've organized this meeting *en masse* to thrash out a modus operandi for dealing with these thugs and it's very important we all show up. Besides, we can take the opportunity to catch up on old times."

Baraldi was referring to their old friendship. When Ottoboni was first starting out, Baraldi had bought his first consignment of sweaters and had commissioned more, thereby insuring the first full year's success for the fledgling firm. His motive had been profit, of course, but he knew he could always count on Ottoboni's sense of gratitude.

With a heavy, reluctant sigh, the Moor of Venice said, "O.K. I'll be there for the meeting tomorrow night. But I'm returning to Venice the next day."

"As you like. I look forward to seeing you again, old friend."

The meeting was being held in the showroom of Maria Teresa di Montenapoleone. Very quickly it became apparent that nothing of any real moment would occur at the meeting and that it would a) last a long time and b) be a very great bore. Someone—Ottoboni couldn't remember who, his mind had long since wandered from the meeting—suggested they build bunkers and underground passageways in Bel Reame. This way they could go about their business without having to ever go aboveground.

201

The Empress, a.k.a. Filippo Ranetti, suggested a collective tax on everyone in Bel Reame to pay the kidnappers so as to defang them before they could act. Kind of a pre-ransom.

Ottoboni, momentarily paying attention when this idea came up, said, "Forget it. Every two-bit hood in Italy would demand a payment. We'd go bankrupt."

Ranetti, who was quite attached to his idea, hissed, "You've always been mingy where money was concerned."

Ottoboni dismissed him with a scornful glance and the comment, "Asshole."

Ranetti had gotten quite worked up over the exchange and retorted, "You're famous for pinching your pennies, you skinflint."

He'd balled his hands into fists and would have physically attacked Ottoboni, except he remembered that Ottoboni had made a name for himself once in the boxing ring. He unballed his fists.

This kind of nonsense went on for hour after inconclusive hour. If there was a final decision at all, it was every man (woman, and other) for himself.

"I'm not worried," Ottoboni had said to Maria Teresa at one point. "It's very difficult to kidnap someone in Venice."

After the meeting they all adjourned to Maria Teresa's villa for cocktails and snacks.

Ranetti came up to Ottoboni to apologize. In a conciliatory mood, Ottoboni said, "Actually your idea wasn't half bad."

"Really? You really think so?" Ranetti slurped up the compliment as if it were the first he had ever received. Wishing to escape, Ottoboni said, "Excuse me," and raced over to his old friend, the Little Lord.

"It's as you said," he said, looking around the room. "Bel Reame is here in force, the only two missing that I can see are Irone and Diovisi. Are they feuding again?"

"Worse than ever. They are avoiding each other at all costs."

"I've never seen such a case of professional jealousy. This has been going on for years."

"This time, it's more complicated. Diovisi bribed Ciaccio's

202

latest lover to leave him causing Ciaccio to collapse and go off for a sleep cure."

Ottoboni generally hated gossip; he felt it cheapened him just to listen to it. But this one sounded especially tantalizing. Encouragingly he murmured, "Hmm, how interesting."

So the Little Lord told him everything, much of it nowhere near the truth—a lot had to be based on conjecture. But the broad general outline of the story wasn't too far off from the facts. All the principals had maintained an iron silence, so the more inventive members of Bel Reame simply filled in the gaps with a lively helping of imagination.

The story had only been glimpsed in tiny bits and pieces, but enough had come to light to whet everyone's appetite for the full story. Ottoboni, mentally off in his eyrie in Venice, listened, feeling totally out of things.

"Is the guy at least handsome?" he asked about Rick.

"Gorgeous. A positive Adonis. What I wouldn't give to share his bed," the Little Lord sighed.

"That good-looking, huh?"

"You wouldn't understand, being straight."

"Don't be silly, of course I understand. It's only in a crowd like this that my being straight is so noticeable."

"It's beyond old-fashioned, it's positively atavistic."

Actually, the Moor of Venice rather enjoyed his special status in the fashion world where all the men were gay and all the women bisexual. He even felt a certain sense of mission in a gathering such as the present one—he was the token straight.

A handsome waiter walked by. The Little Lord followed. Ottoboni walked over to the terrace windows, wondering how soon he could leave without insulting his hostess. He was palpably missing his favorite armchair, his glass of wine, his cigar—his nightly ritual.

He joined a group in which the Handsome Priest, Tatino Faveri, was holding forth. Faveri was looking especially frail these days—Ottoboni hadn't seen him for several years and was amaz-

ed how altered he looked. He was still handsome, but his skin seemed worn, inelastic. There was an air of unhealthy pallor about him.
Of course, he held his trademark—Jack Daniel's neat—in a glass
in one hand, while gesticulating with the other that held his omnipresent cigarette.

When Ottoboni joined the group, Faveri smiled a warm
acknowledgment. As soon as he finished what he was saying—it
was a harangue against a competitor, of course, one who was
underhanded and unscrupulous, no less—he turned to Ottoboni
and said, "Here's a sight for sore eyes. How good it is to see you,
and looking so well. You must get to Milan more—" Here he broke
off. Suddenly sweat broke out all over his forehead. He went very
pale. And then he was totally overcome by a paroxysm of coughing
that was so spectacular it threatened to stop the party in its tracks.
His coughing made him drop his glass of Jack Daniel's. His face
turned a livid red, then a ghastly pale white.

"Someone get a glass of water," a voice rang out.

Ottoboni grabbed onto Faveri's arm and tried leading him
to a nearby armchair.

Catching his breath finally, Faveri said, "Thanks, I think it's
passed. Someday I'll give up these goddam cigarettes. I know
they're no good for one's health."

Concerned, Ottoboni asked, "Are you sure you're all right?"

Weak, but visibly improved, Faveri said, "Thanks for being
so concerned. I think it's just a combination of everything, mostly due to overwork—the new collection is taking everything out
of me. As soon as the collection premieres, I've promised myself
a long—and very well deserved, I might add—rest."

Tatino livened up to the point where he seemed like his old
self and the party sprang back to life.

Bored, Ottoboni wandered around the room, not wishing to
join any group. He overheard snatches of conversation as he moved
about.

"They've finally broken up. They're unhappy about it, but
the kids are thrilled to death."

"He looked at me so strangely when he told me that he was going to Capri for six months to finish the book and I asked what he was reading."

"He dropped her like a hot potato as soon as he met her mother. Is there a word for that kind of rivalry?"

Ottoboni headed toward the kitchen to get a refill. En route, he changed his mind and decided to sneak out as inconspicuously as he could manage.

Damn, the door was blocked by Aldoni Stembiati, a.k.a. the Pipe. Not surprisingly, he held a pipe between his teeth. He claimed it was a gift from the President of Italy. One wag had said, "It's not as good as the Maltese Cross, but it's something."

"It's been ages, Zaco. How have you been?" the Pipe asked.

Annoyed at his foiled escape plan, Ottoboni answered irritably. "Anytime you want to see me, you know where I can be found. I can't help it if I'm a homebody. Look me up the next time you're in Venice. I'm in the book."

"What are you doing now?"

Trying to get out of here, was his thought. Instead, politely he said, "Nothing, why?"

"Then come with me. I'm throwing a party at my place—it starts in about"—looking at his watch—"half an hour ago."

Ottoboni sighed. "The usual crowd?"

"No, a whole different set of faces. All young, all pretty."

"All gay?"

"Don't be silly, of course not. Lots of straights are invited. And there's super coke from Peru."

"What the hell. Lead the way."

The Pipe's house was not in Bel Reame. He had acquired it years before from a bankrupt banker—it was on the outskirts of Milan. Over the years he had restored the place to the point where it now was one of the great villas of Italy.

Although the party was announced to start at ten P.M., in Italy that means that around ten P.M. a guest should start thinking about going to the party. When they arrived at the villa, though it was already ten-thirty there was barely a guest in sight. Stembiati took the opportunity to take Ottoboni on a complete tour of the villa.

There was much to see. The basement, for instance, had been transformed into an art gallery. There were more than 100 pieces of sculpture and painting in the collection, including two Renoirs (albeit early efforts), two Picassos, three Miros and three Picabias. The foyer in the entranceway was lined with photographs—Cartier-Bresson, Brassai, Kertesz among others.

"The greatest piece is in my bedroom," Stembiati said. "A Piero della Francesca. Don't worry, I've got mountains of authentication certificates for it. Its provenance is impeccable. Would you like to see it?"

"Perhaps later, when I could use some stimulation," Ottoboni said. "In Venice, I'm inundated with art all the time as it is."

"I didn't know you were a collector too."

"I'm not, I don't need to be. The entire city of Venice is a museum. All I have to do is go for a stroll and I see enough art to last a lifetime of museum-going."

"That's a very odd attitude to have about art. Since we're both so wealthy, that is. I find, in fact, that I can't truly appreciate a work of art unless I own it."

"Three cheers for your capitalistic mentality."

Stembiati now was quite curious. "Then what, may I ask, do you do with all your money?"

"I really couldn't say. My wife Gina takes care of all that. She has a good head for business and enjoys it."

"Well, if you're satisfied . . . "

"I'm more than satisfied. I'm happy. I don't have to worry about a thing and my life goes along just the way I want it. What more could I ask?"

Totally perplexed, Stembiati decided to change the subject. "What would you like to drink?"

"Some Merlot, if you have it. Otherwise, any dry red would

do."

"I think there's some in the kitchen—the servants like that kind of drink. I'll ask the butler."

The Pipe went in search of the butler, shaking his head in disbelief. Ottoboni dropped into a nearby armchair.

They were all alike, he thought, meaning all the Bel Reame successes. They'd all come up from poor backgrounds. The second they got their hand on real bucks, and the money started rolling in, they started spending it in the same way. They'd pay an arm and two legs for paintings, drawings and the like. They'd shell out small fortunes for antique furniture. Knowing they were wealthy wasn't enough, they needed the tangible proofs high-price collectibles provided. Some of them, amusingly enough, played the hometown patron and subsidized a soccer team from whatever small town they'd escaped from in the first place. It gave them some kind of satisfaction to see their firm's name on the backs of the provincial jocks.

Ottoboni didn't exclude himself from this analysis. He too had clawed his way up, had gained fame and fortune. He thought his sweaters were attractive enough, but he had no explanation why they caught on so spectacularly. He held on to a sense of modesty at least—he didn't think of himself as a genius, as many in Bel Reame did.

Stembiati returned with the wine and Ottoboni poured himself a drink. The guests were now beginning to arrive in large numbers. Stembiati hadn't lied—many of the women were young and beautiful.

Now, Ottoboni, like everyone else in Bel Reame, had a deep, dark secret he daren't reveal. He loved his wife Gina, had always been faithful to her and still was. If Bel Reame ever found that out it would cause a scandal. In its eyes, the ultimate perversion was fidelity. All the world of fashion was based on a talent for flair, a sense of style. Fidelity was a rebuke to that. It implied a lack of imagination, a lack of the sense of human complexity and possibility.

Ottoboni was very careful to guard his secret from Bel Reame. The reason, in fact, he accepted the invitation to this party, although he would infinitely rather be alone at home with his wife, was to give the appearance of a man who'd broken loose from his leash. He would circulate among the guests and flirt enough so that word could get back that, now he was free from his wife's watchful eye, he was reverting to a more natural state; in short, he was tomcatting about.

He zeroed in on a woman who was quite tall, quite thin, but had rich brown eyes and sensually full lips. She looked as stupid as she was beautiful. It would be a perfect cover.

By the time he wended his way through the throng to the part of the room he'd seen her in she was nowhere in sight. Wineglass in hand, he wandered about.

On the second floor he came upon a beautiful woman lying on a sofa half-naked, sucking up some coke with a silver spoon to her nose. She smiled and held out the spoon invitingly. He smiled back and waved her offer away. "Perhaps later," he said.

He opened a door to find himself in a bedroom. He recognized the statuesque beauty he was in search of. She was moaning in pleasure on the bed, crouching, as someone was fucking her doggy fashion. Then, about to turn away, he noticed his host off in a corner. Stembiati was sitting in an armchair, his pants down around his ankles. He was jacking off to the spectacle on the bed. Ottoboni's intrusion didn't cause him to miss a stroke.

Waving Ottoboni over, he called out, "Come watch the show. It's fabulous!"

Ottoboni had had enough for one night—for several nights. He decided it was time to leave. He went over to Stembiati and whispered, "Thanks for a wonderful party. Look me up the next time you're in Venice." He couldn't tell if Stembiati heard him, and if he heard him, understood. All he did was nod his head once.

He threaded his way down the hall and downstairs. The party was in full swing. It was wall to wall people, all trying hard to have a good time.

At the door, Ottoboni bumped into a guy entering, wearing shorts and carrying a small pail in his hand. On further inspection, the pail held a goldfish swimming merrily in small circles.

"Hi there. I'm Duke Fabio de Fandoli," the man in the shorts said. "And this," indicating the goldfish, "is Don Felipe, my favorite goldfish."

"Poor thing," Ottoboni said.

"Who, my goldfish?" the Duke asked enraged.

"No, you," Ottoboni said as he elbowed his way out of the house.

The mugginess of the city hit him full in the face, but he was so glad to be free of the party that he breathed it in in huge drafts. He walked toward the park, looking for a cab. Never had he missed his beloved Venice so much, even the smell of the canals was poetry compared to Milan.

He resolved never to come back to Milan, not even if a million-dollar contract depended on it. Anyone wants me, they know where to reach me. I'm in the book.

He finally got a cab. "Where to?" the cabbie asked.

He gave the name of his hotel. As soon as he got back—it wasn't all that late—he'd call Gina and wish her good night. He'd tell her he loved her and what time his train would get him into Venice tomorrow.

Chapter 21

*I*nna glared at Diana, a sullen look on her face. Diana felt like giving her a good hard slap in the face. She was determined that, in her battle for Inna's reform, she would come out the victor. She would not lose this fight. She had to save her niece from her own self-destructive impulses.

Inna sat in the armchair, silent, as she had been for the last hour, as Diana walked up and back reasoning, arguing, trying her damndest to persuade Inna to reform.

"I'm offering you a priceless opportunity, Inna, don't you see? When I started out, I had to do everything for myself, I had no loving aunt to ease the way for me. I went through a hell of a lot before I was able to even get a toe on the ladder. I'm offering to spare you all that and more."

Inna looked up and, with the oddest look on her face, said,

"The difference, among other things, is that you cared."

Diana came to an abrupt halt. She was prepared to deal with all kinds of arguments, but this one—indifference—was furthest from her mind.

"And you don't care?"

Inna shrugged. "I don't think I care in that all-consuming passionate way of yours. Certainly not enough to give up my freedom."

"Freedom? What freedom? Freedom to snort coke? Freedom to screw any passing stranger? That's not freedom."

"It's what gives me pleasure."

"No one's against pleasure. What are you saying? Do you want to end up like Fuxia—she wasn't against pleasure either. I've seen too many young women end up like her, not in *Vogue*, but in a morgue."

Inna's voice rose an entire octave. "I think you're morbid. Would you stop bringing up Fuxia?"

"She was your friend. She loved you. I don't think Fuxia wanted to die the way she did. She wanted everything she could get out of life. She wanted success. I don't want to see you end up the same way. Inna, I love you."

Diana felt that she had finally broken through to Inna; it was the mention of Fuxia's tragic waste *and* Diana's love that did it.

Inna got up and came over to Diana. "Let's try a sort of compromise."

"Fine," Diana said. "What do you propose?"

"I'll work for you—purely on a trial basis. I'm not promising anything. What precisely do you want from me?"

"It's very simple really. I want you to buckle down and concentrate on work. Until October, when the collection premieres, I want you to give up drink, drugs and staying out all night. You'll be surprised how easy it is to stop all that."

"Are you sure?"

"Of course I'm sure. I've snorted coke on occasion. But I do it to clear my mind so it improves my thinking when I work. I'm in control that way. I can take it or leave it."

"Maybe it won't be so easy for me."

"It will be, I'm sure. For one thing, you're still so young, you have the resiliency of youth. Also I'm counting on hooking you—hooking you with work, that is. Once you get involved, I'm hoping you will begin to care—to use your word. Then you'll see how stupid all drugs are—expensive indulgences, nothing more."

"How far along is the collection?"

"It's a bit tough to say—we're getting there. Kao has put up all the necessary funds. He's also sending me three Japanese stylists and five designers. He says they're really sharp, they know how to follow instructions perfectly."

"When is the show?"

"In October. No one's expecting it. It will hit Bel Reame for an absolute loop."

"Not even Irone?"

"I had to tell him, he's the one exception. No one else knows. He even wished me good luck. What a gentleman he is."

"O.K. You've won me over. I'll give you my all—until the show."

"And after that?"

"Don't press your luck, Diana. For now be satisfied."

Diana threw her arms around Inna and hugged her. "I really do love you, Inna. I want to see you happy."

"Would you describe yourself as being happy, Diana?"

Diana thought of the collection, daily taking on more and more meaning in her life. Then she thought of Kao, helpful, considerate and supportive. Then she thought of Andrea, who had returned to his garret room just the night before. Andrea had returned in a sulky mood, in a funk so deep he barely said hello. Smiling, but crossing her fingers behind her back just in case, she said, "Yes, I'm happy."

Diana was having a good deal of trouble with Andrea. The heart of the problem was that he balked at the idea of sharing her affections, or at least her body, with someone else. He wanted Diana to give up everything for him. She admired his romantic attitude but she also saw it as unreal, inapplicable to the circumstances of her life. Twenty years ago, maybe, she might have abandoned her ambitions and thrown her lot in with his. But she'd worked too hard, too long, come too close to realizing her career dreams to act like a love-smitten teenager.

"When's Kao coming back?" he asked her.

"The day of the show, not before. So we have until October at least to be together, you and I."

Sneering, he said, "Thanks for that. I'm grateful for any crumb from your table you care to toss my way. When's the marriage?"

Diana gave Andrea a hug. God his flesh felt good. "It's not as if we've talked about it that much. We haven't set a date, if that's what you mean. Maybe there won't even be a marriage."

"Whether or not you marry, that still doesn't preclude your having sex with him, does it? You do have sex with him?"

"If I didn't know you better I'd think you were jealous."

"Goddam it, Diana, of course I'm jealous. It drives me crazy to think of the two of you in bed."

Diana was oddly moved by his jealousy. It was so direct, so uncomplicated. In the world of Bel Reame, where hopping into bed with someone was as common as talking about the weather, jealousy was virtually an unknown emotion.

This was one of the reasons Diana was in love with Andrea—he still clung to the old-fashioned virtues: things like truth-telling, sexual fidelity, devotion to one person. It wouldn't surprise her to find out he went to confession every week.

"I love you," she whispered. "I've never loved anyone in my whole life the way I love you."

"You haven't really answered my question. Do you and Kao go to bed together?"

"Yes, of course we do. You'll learn, Andrea, as we all must, that nothing comes free—everything has a price."

"How do you think I feel about the matter of your infidelity?"

"Technically, *caro*, my infidelity is with you—you came into my life after I'd already worked out this deal with Kao. He's the one who should be jealous."

"Why couldn't you keep your relationship with him on a purely business level?"

"Business, as you call it, often doesn't work so simply. Yes, Kao is backing my firm, but I'm not the only good investment in the world. He's backing me also because he really likes me, maybe in his cool fashion, he loves me."

"Does he make it a practice to sleep with every new investment?"

"Don't be snotty. In his world—and mine too, at least until I met you—one doesn't think in terms of 'mixing business and pleasure.' They meld and run into each other until they're indistinguishable."

"Where does that leave me?"

"Andrea, you know I love you. Can't you see things at all from my point of view?"

"You're not exactly poor, why do you need him anyway?"

"You have no idea how much it costs to launch a new fashion house."

"Then give it up, Diana. You've still got your job with Irone—I could get some kind of job. We could manage."

"You refuse to understand. I can't break it off. This fashion house is my lifelong dream come true."

Andrea extricated himself from her embrace and got out of bed. He was getting dressed.

"Andrea, can't we work out some kind of compromise?"

"There's no compromising on this issue. Either give up Kao or lose me."

"Be reasonable, Andrea. Kao spends maybe all of twenty days a year in Milan."

"Decide. Him or me."

"Oh Andrea, please . . . "

215

He opened the closet door. There was a valise, clearly already packed.

"Kao or me. This time I mean it for keeps. I won't be coming back."

Diana got off the bed and put on a robe. Sitting there naked made her feel that much more vulnerable. A quiet anger was building in her over his ultimatum. "I will not be held hostage this way," she said.

"That's it, then."

"I'm begging you, Andrea. Bend a little, I'm not asking you to compromise a lot, just a little."

"Out of the question. No compromises."

"I'm begging you not to do anything foolish. The bad thing about ultimatums is you can't take them back. Stay, please. We'll work it out."

"I said it and I mean it, no compromises."

Diana in a burst of fury went over to the valise and practically threw it at Andrea. "Then go, get out of my life. I got along without you for nearly forty years. I think I can manage to survive without you for the next forty."

Although his lips were quivering, he didn't hesitate. He picked up the valise and headed for the door. "Good luck with your collection," he called over his back as he left.

He's left and come back twice already, she thought. He'll be back again. No, this time she realized was for keeps. He would not be coming back any more.

She went and threw herself on the bed, ready to give herself over to a self-pitying crying jag. But the tears wouldn't come.

She realized she needed solace from something stronger than the relief provided by a good cry. She ran downstairs and got some coke. She snorted two good lines and instantly felt calmer. She needed something more. Something that would put her totally over into the calm oblivion she sought. Grabbing a bottle of gin, she unscrewed the top and took a hefty slug from the bottle. She found the raw gin taste vile, but a few minutes later its effect was being

216

felt throughout her body. It boosted and enhanced the coke—every fiber in her body was pleasantly numb.

She went and knocked on Inna's door. Inna was in bed reading a fashion magazine.

"Come on," Diana said. "We have work to do."

Inna glanced at the clock. It was midnight. "I'm about ready for bed."

"Forget it. I'm overflowing with ideas and I need you to help me."

"That could be fun," Inna said, getting up.

"It is. Creating elegant and beautiful things is the most wonderful thing on earth. It's a high greater than any drug—or any man—could provide."

For two solid weeks Diana worked virtually non-stop. At the most, she slipped in about two or three hours' sleep a night. Otherwise she was at the worktable all the time. Inna, the stylists, the designers periodically threw in the towel and collapsed for a day or two. Never Diana—she was indefatigable.

Of course she had a little help from her friends—if coke and gin can be called friends. Whenever they seemed to flag, there was the occasional upper to boost her along to the next plateau.

Now and then she thought of Andrea and felt a stab in the pit of her stomach, but mostly she dismissed thoughts of him with an act of will and returned to the design she was working on. She was as wired as it was possible to be, as taut as a violin's E string.

By the beginning of the third week, Inna voiced her alarm. "You keep it up at this pace and you're going to kill yourself," she said.

"Don't worry about me, Inna. Work is all the world for me, it's good for me. If I didn't have my work, I'd perish from the boredom."

"Work is one thing, but this pace you're going at is maniacal."

"As soon as the show premiers, I'll take some time off for a good rest. Of course, not too much time; there's always the next show to worry about."

"Your pupils are completely dilated. It's very noticeable."

"I can handle it, I told you. The important thing is that *you* keep away from the drugs."

"I gave you my word. I've been clean ever since."

"It's quite different for me. I'm mature enough to handle the stuff."

"I don't know if you're all that mature."

Diana laughed. "It looks like our roles are getting reversed."

"I'm just worried about you."

"There's no need to worry. I'm not ready to be put out to pasture quite yet."

Inna backed off. She was able to see first hand how easy it was to get completely—passionately—caught up in a work project. Inna's enthusiasm was growing daily. She hadn't thought of having sex in nearly two full weeks now.

Diana was in a stupor, something resembling sleep, but heavier, full of cotton batting. It was one of those rare times she'd lain down for a couple hours of rest. At first, it sounded so far away, she incorporated the ringing into her dream. The ringing persisted until it broke through her haze and she realized it was the phone.

It was Alvise Mittaglia calling. He sounded oddly restrained. He was calling with bad news.

"Tatino Faveri's dead," he announced lugubriously.

"Faveri? Our Handsome Priest is dead? What kind of a joke is this, Alvise?"

"No joke. I just came from the hospital. I know how fond of him you were. You're the first one I called."

"He wasn't old or anything. What did he die of?"

"It was kind of a three-way race. Between the way he drank like a fish and smoked like a chimney and whored around constantly. People were actually taking bets, which would give out first, his lungs, his liver or his immune system."

"He was that ill?"

218

"It was a photo finish—they have to do an autopsy yet. Whether it was lung cancer, cirrhosis of the liver or AIDS—they need an official cause to put on the death certificate."

Since Lana and Martita had recently arrived in Milan, they had never known Faveri. However, they knew that his funeral would be an important event—all of Bel Reame would be out in force. Knowing how well they looked in black, they decided to avoid the church services entirely and arrived early at the cemetery to get a good spot so they would be noticed by all the VIPs of Bel Reame.

Their instincts proved right. For the moment, waiting for the funeral procession to arrive, they looked like two forlorn ravens. They had gotten Giancarlo Ferré to make their outfits for them and he outdid himself—in 36 hours their outfits were done. Lana was especially pleased about hers—how the muttonchop sleeves played against the smooth deep tan of her arms.

A gray Rolls pulled up through the gates. The chauffeur, in all-white livery, got out and opened the back door. Ubaldo Baraldi emerged, sleek and elegant in a three-piece suit of black alpaca.

A blue Ferrari B.B. coupe pulled up next. Two handsome men in their thirties, both in blue-linen double-breasted suits, got out. Neither of the women recognized them. They were silk manufacturers from Como.

Now a steady stream of cars and people started pouring through the gates. Many of the women—all dressed in the most fashionable black outfits imaginable—were young and beautiful. Lana thought, The competition is fierce around here.

"You look great, *cara*." Lana and Martita overheard many conversations as groups of people milled around. "You look great too, *cara*. You carry your age so well."

"Black is a divine color. If I had my way my entire wardrobe would be in black."

"Where'd you get that tan, it's fabulous."

"Marbella. Would you believe that I was playing golf this

morning? I came as soon as I heard."

"Poor Tatino. I was floored when I heard."

"I cried all night. Look what it did to my face."

"It was all so sudden."

"The rumor I heard was that he died of AIDS."

"So now it's in Italy. Fucking may go completely out of style, like the miniskirt."

"Whatever else you can say about Faveri, he was an absolute master at his profession."

"Oh, we all learned from him."

"Everybody's here, have you noticed?"

"I heard even Irone and Diovisi were at the church. They didn't acknowledge each other but still, on an important occasion like this, I'm glad to see them put aside their feud for a couple of hours."

"Look over there. Valentino came up from Rome."

"And to think that just last night I was going to give Faveri a call—we were such good friends."

"You'll never hear a nasty word about Faveri from me, but somehow it's just like him to die in this beastly weather. Couldn't he wait till it cooled off a bit?"

"They don't call these the dog days for nothing."

"Look, there's the King of Furs, Ranetti."

"How can you even mention furs in this kind of weather?"

"The fashion world is losing one of its brightest jewels."

"Must you always resort to such hyperbole?"

"There's Paolo Boggi. The king of the discount trade. They say even a bag lady could afford one of his originals."

At that moment, eight men on magnificent chargers appeared at the gates. Everybody was agape at the splendor. Finally they found out it was a gesture from Baraldi, he had hired on eight bodyguards to protect himself against potential kidnappers. The bodyguards looked great on their horses—rented for the day from a local stable.

Finally the hearse appeared, gliding majestically into the

cemetery. People parted, creating a narrow path for the long vehicle to drive through. The sounds now were nonverbal—the appearance of the hearse had sobered the crowd to silence. All one heard was the clipclop of the horses and the swish swish of yards of taffeta and lace as the crowd edged toward the grave.

Four hefty men, all in black down to their gloves, removed the coffin from the hearse and carried it to the gravesite.

Although there was a multitude of black handkerchiefs in evidence, dabbing ever so prettily at eyes and noses, one would have had to have the ears of a bat to catch a sound remotely resembling a sob.

Faveri was laid to rest.

Chapter 22

The pile made by the mail on Diovisi's desk was its usual size—quite large. When he came upon the oversize envelope with no return address, he put it aside, saving it for last. Maybe it would be a pleasant surprise.

He waded through the pile stoically, dutifully. Finally he got through it and reached for the mysterious envelope. He tore it open. It was filled with photographs. For the head of a design firm, receiving photos in the mail was the most common of experiences. But this batch of photos was unique.

No sound of surprise—or shock—came from him. He went through several of the photos—there seemed to be several dozen altogether—in a state of stupefied shock. They were of his highly guarded and protected new collection. There was the black-and-white silk with the showy belt. There was the knitwear jacket with large flowers and cuffed sleeves. There was the pink gabardine with asymmetrical buttons.

It was all there, as far as he could tell—his entire new collection. His best collection yet. Ruined.

At first he thought it might be a mindless joke by some assistant, but he dismissed the idea almost immediately. He buzzed his secretary. She came in.

Holding up the envelope, he asked, "When did this arrive?"

"It was part of this morning's mail."

What else was she going to say? He dismissed her.

He leafed through the photos, not believing what he was seeing. The depth of the maliciousness involved was breathtaking. Whoever did this knew his victim well. He knew how the collection of photos would devastate Diovisi. Because it came anonymously, Diovisi would have no idea who sent it. Much worse, he would have no idea how many people had seen it, had already begun to copy it. All his most brilliant ideas, the months and months of planning and execution, absolutely out the window. The entire collection could be considered down the drain. He would have to start over again from scratch, create an entirely new line.

To let off some steam he got up and started pacing about. He picked up a paperweight and threw it against a wall. Damn, damn, damn. Who would be malicious enough to do such a thing? Of course he had enemies—in the fashion world, every competitor could be considered an enemy. Perhaps it was an inside job. Even if that were the case, which he doubted—he implicitly trusted his staff—there was no flushing out the villain. It would only consume time and time was one thing he couldn't spare now.

Whoever it was who had done all this mischief would get his comeuppance sometime, but for now Diovisi had to think practically. He'd show them. No one alive could work better and longer under pressure than Diovisi. He might be temporarily down but he wasn't out. He'd create a whole new collection.

He hit the phones, summoning his entire staff, telling them to drop everything and get to his office post haste. They were all in town. Within an hour they were all gathered in his office.

Diovisi circulated the photos of the sketches of the entire collection. "It's obvious that the entire collection is now an open secret. I've been betrayed!"

This created a great hubbub, but Diovisi silenced them all with a gesture. "I'm not accusing any of you. I know you're all loyal. Here's the important point. We have to start over again, we have to prepare another collection, and do it in record time. We have to work our asses to the bone. We have a little bit of leeway— we can reschedule the show a few weeks later in October. Needless to say, all your hard work will be rewarded. I'm preparing to double your salaries and give you all an extra bonus at the end. But I warn you: You're going to have to work like slaves. If you get two hours sleep a night you'll be lucky. I'll be making the exact same sacrifices. If any of you doesn't feel up to it for whatever reason, now's your chance to bow out."

As Diovisi had hoped and expected, no one got up to leave. His people were truly loyal. He'd always treated them well.

Later, sitting alone with his sketchpad, his mind kept returning, almost against his will, to the mystery of the photos. He entertained the idea of hiring private detectives, but abandoned the idea as unnecessarily cumbersome. He didn't need a troop of detectives infesting his workshop asking questions, getting in the way.

All his thoughts on the subject were rendered academic at midnight. Just as the clock was striking the hour, the phone rang. Of all people it was the Big Turk.

"Have you had a nice day, Lorenzo?" Ciaccio asked in a voice that was oleaginously smooth and insinuating.

In a flash, it all came clear. Diovisi, putting on a brave front, answered, "Not bad. Why do you ask?"

"We can put aside all pretense, Lorenzo. I know better. You've had one of the worst days of your life. How did you like my little joke?"

"So it was you."

"Were you in any doubt?"

"I was. I really didn't think you would stoop this low, you

bastard."

"Have you any idea what it cost me to get Rick back?"

"A pretty penny, I'm sure."

"The money wasn't the half of it. I was thinking more about the emotional cost."

"I'll say this for you—when you retaliate, you don't kid around."

"I certainly won't use your models. Though all things considered, they're not half bad."

"Who else knows about this theft of yours?"

"As the saying goes, that's for me to know and for you to find out."

"Up yours, Ciaccio."

"That's no attitude to take. We're even now. It's time for the dust to settle."

"You're probably right. Let's declare an armistice."

"Let's."

"Until the next outbreak of hostilities."

"If that's the way you want to act, it's O.K. with me."

Irone hung up. Diovisi stared off into space, his mind reeling in all directions. Ciaccio had no sense of proportion, that was the problem. When Diovisi had convinced Rick to disappear, it was in the nature of a prank, nothing more. Who could have predicted that Ciaccio had gotten himself bitten by the love bug and that he would go into a total tailspin, like some melodramatic teenager.

First things first. The priority was the new collection. He would have to produce a new one, and goddam it, it would be even better than its predecessor. Luckily, his mind was overflowing with new, even more original ideas. In a way he ought to be thankful to Ciaccio for stimulating him like this. There was nothing he liked more in the world than working on new ideas, coming up with new concepts, giving his imagination free rein. The extra costs—all the salaries, the new models—would come to a tidy fortune. But he shrugged the costs off as the least of his problems. In fact, Sam

226

Violante was due back from America tomorrow, and he'd be bringing a vast new source of financing.

Ciaccio was laughing uncontrollably. Rick looked at him as if he'd taken leave of his senses. Ciaccio would laugh hysterically, then get control of himself, then in a few minutes would start laughing again.

"Stop that!" Rick exclaimed. "You're getting on my nerves." Ciaccio tried, but he couldn't stop. Rick grabbed hold of his arm, spun him around and, in exasperation, slapped him. This made Ciaccio stop. It took him a while to calm down.

"What is so goddam funny anyhow? Let me in on it. I'd like a good laugh too."

"I called Diovisi. Oh, how I wish I could have seen his face when he first opened that envelope."

"You're not making any sense. What is this all about?"

"I finally got back at him for sending you away to L.A."

Rick was annoyed. "Are you still dwelling on that? I thought you'd forgotten all about it by now."

"Now, I can forget about it. I had to write the final chapter, but now the book is done."

"I don't pretend to understand you. I love Italy and the Italians, but just when I think I'm about to grasp the true nature of the place and the people, it all becomes even more incomprehensible. For instance, I have to turn to you to ask when my wedding is."

"I'm so sorry, I thought you knew already. In three weeks. By September the weather will be more bearable and everybody will be back in town. You wouldn't believe the size of Sabina's guest list."

"She's great. I really like her," Rick said.

Suspicion dripping from every pore, Ciaccio asked, "What do you mean, you like her?"

"Just that. I think she's nice. It'll be fun going on a honeymoon with her."

"Don't forget, I'll be tagging along as well. If you've got any designs on my sister, forget it."

"I believe you're a little jealous, Ciaccio. Of your own sister, no less. By the way, have you decided where we're going on our honeymoon?"

"I have a castle in Scotland that will be perfect in September. If Sabina gets horny, she'll have to find herself a gameskeeper, like Lady Chatterly. I have no intention of sharing you with her."

Rick smiled to himself. Ciaccio had no idea that that was precisely what he was doing. Just to goad Ciaccio, he asked, "What would you do, if you found Sabina and me between the sheets?"

"I'd beat the living daylights out of you, that's what."

"You're getting a little confused, *caro*. You're the one who gets beat up in this family."

That night Rick had beat Ciaccio with his belt had been revelatory for Ciaccio. It brought him a new, exquisite pleasure, one he could never get enough of. Now, at the mention of his being on the receiving end, his eyes gleamed with anticipation.

Seeing this, Rick asked, "Would you prefer my hands or my belt?"

"Bare hands, on my ass, *caro*," Ciaccio sighed as he turned over on his stomach.

Jenny was nervous enough to give birth to kittens. Sam Violante, having just returned from America, was in conference with Diovisi. She'd noticed him enter but was too far away to call out. She followed and now she was sitting in Diovisi's anteroom, tormenting herself.

Maybe he'd forgotten all about her, or worse, she was a pleasant dalliance for an evening, one he never meant to pursue. Or maybe he'd met someone he much preferred in the course of his trip to America.

All the possibilities that occurred to her were dire and filled with unhappiness. Several of the other models had wandered over to shoot the breeze with her but she seemed so distracted they drifted away puzzled by her uncommunicative state.

Rumors were flying all over the place this morning. The atmosphere was thick with tension. She had heard that they were doing over the whole collection, but she dismissed that as too wild a rumor to pay attention to. Besides, she had other things on her mind.

It wasn't till two in the afternoon that Sam finally emerged from Diovisi's office. Please, God, just let him smile, at least that. Her heart was beating wildly as he strode across the anteroom. He noticed her. He smiled.

She ran over to him.

"Hi, Jenny," he said.

Her legs were trembling—she hadn't felt like this since the seventh-grade crush she had on her math teacher, Mr. Gorman.

"Welcome back," she managed to get out somehow.

Prompting her, he said, "Welcome back—what?"

"Welcome back, Sam."

He took her hand in his. "Have you forgotten all about me so soon?"

"Oh, Sam. All I've been thinking about these last several days is you. I was afraid you wouldn't come back."

"I've been thinking about you too. Can we go to your place?"

"When? Now?"

"Right now sounds fine. I want to make love to you and this office doesn't have the right atmosphere somehow."

Jenny nodded, her face beaming with happiness.

Sex with Sam was wonderful—he was soft and gentle when he had to be, hard and strong when that was called for. Perhaps that was one of the major ways to separate out the men from the boys, Jenny thought, as she cast her mind back over innumerable experiences with callow young men. She snuggled up to Sam's chest, feeling warm and protected.

"I love you, Jenny."

"Really? I'm not just another fling, another one-night stand?"

229

"From now on, it's just the two of us. We're a team. I'd marry you in a minute if I weren't already married."

Jenny's heart skipped a beat. Sam hadn't referred to a wife, never even hinted at the existence of one.

"You didn't tell me you were married."

"It never came up. In New York. I've also got four kids, a son who's a year older than you in fact. Don't let any of this throw you, Jenny. I couldn't get a divorce because of the Catholic thing. And as for sex, ever since my wife hit menopause—it must be a good ten years now—all she does is go to church and involve herself in charity work. There's no sex between us. As far as I'm concerned, you're my woman."

"Oh, Sam, how I love you. This morning, waiting outside Diovisi's office . . . "

"That reminds me. We've got some big problems there. The collection's been stolen—all of Diovisi's sketches."

Suddenly it all came back to Jenny. She'd meant to bring up the unsavory incident with the coke as soon as she got together with Sam, but she'd been waylaid. Now was the time to bring it up.

"The evening we were together, just before you went back to New York?"

"What about it?"

"First answer me this. Did you leave any kind of package in my car?"

"What are you talking about? What package?"

"A huge package of cocaine. The cops stopped me and found it right away."

Violante, suspicion breaking out all over his face, said, "I've done a lot of shady things in my life, but I've never messed with drugs."

"Then how did the package get in my car?"

"Let's take this one step at a time. What happened after they pulled you in to the station?"

She told him everything, leaving out no details. She told him about meeting Giovanna, about the arrest in front of her house, about an old acquaintance turning up to bail her out, about the fact he had asked a favor of her in return.

"What kind of favor?"

"He wanted me to photograph Diovisi's sketches. He gave me a miniature camera to shoot the pictures with."

"And you did it?"

"I had no choice, really. I thought you had accidentally left the cocaine in my car. I had to protect you, don't you see?"

Violante caressed her. "I love you, Jenny. But boy, were you set up. It was a booby trap."

"What do you mean?"

"Five'll get you ten, Irone was behind it all. He and Diovisi are constantly needling away at each other. It's too long to go into. Anyhow, the thing I don't like, don't like at all in fact, is how they used you. What's the name of the guy who so obligingly turned up to bail you out?"

"Ugo Varanni, a real lowlife. He owns the Image Agency."

Violante got up from the bed. It was impossible to read the look on his face.

"Where's the phone?" he asked.

"In there. Next to the TV."

He walked into the next room to get to the phone. Jenny admired his taut figure as it moved through space. He must exercise, she thought, in admiration for the excellent state of his body.

In the other room, Violante was in conversation, but he was speaking in too low a voice for her to catch any of it. Jenny lay back against the pillows, aglow with the thoughts of someone newly in love.

It was dawn, the early dawn where the light is closer to gray than anything else. There was the slightest hint of a snap in the air, portent of the longed-for, pleasant autumn weather yet to arrive that would relieve everyone from the oppressive mugginess and heat.

Varanni had won a not-small fortune that night at Campione

and although it had been almost twenty-four hours since he'd slept, there was a bounce of joy in his step as he approached his new Maserati. Everything was—finally—coming up roses for him.

The only problem was Giovanna, who, still anxious and worried as ever, was driving him up the wall with her constant whining. He had just about had enough of her. Her problem was, she had no capacity for joy, for enjoying the good things of life. He had half a mind to pack her off to the provincial town she'd come from and walk away from her altogether. He'd find another—younger, more agreeable, more suitable—woman to fill his needs.

He was lost in admiration of the Maserati, its lines so sleek, so elegant. It had been his dream to own one, and finally his dream had come true. But there would be more, many more realized dreams from now on. The Maserati was just the start.

Out of sheer morning gladness he found himself unconsciously whistling as he approached the car. He decided he'd go to a luxurious hotel for the night, and pamper himself. His winnings made a hefty bundle in his pants pocket—in addition, that is, to all the Swiss francs he had been able to stuff into his wallet.

As he opened the door to the Maserati, he noticed two men on the other side of the street get out of a blue Ritmo.

They were approaching him. They looked like foreigners—Americans, to judge by their clothing. Probably they were lost, looking for directions. One of them began to smile at him.

"Excuse me," he said courteously as he came up to Varanni.

Varanni returned the smile. "Yes? What is it I can do for you?"

Although it was only a small bag of sand, it felt like a brick had clobbered him right behind his left ear. That was his impression as he lost consciousness. When he came to, he found himself in the Ritmo—handcuffed.

"Listen," he said, panic rising from his stomach into his throat, "if it's money you're after, you're in luck. I've got a bundle on me. You can have it all."

One of the two men, the non-smiler, said, "Tell him to shut up. If not, I'll sap him again."

232

"Signor Varanni, you pulled a fast one on a certain woman—a good friend of ours—and had her steal Diovisi's designs."

"It was work done for someone else—I only carried out what was contracted to me."

"Ain't that always the way! The big fish swim away free and safe, while the little fish get gobbled up."

The Ritmo was driving along the water. Varanni realized this was it, his number was up. There was no use pleading with these guys—they too were fulfilling a contract. An icy chill ran down his spine. Goddam Giovanna, he thought, she was right all along.

Chapter 23

By the second week of September, everybody was back in Milan. Paolo Sgargaglia was behind the wheel of his new Rolls-Royce. Popi Giccheri was back from Saratoga where he pursued his interest in horse races and, as the more catty members of Bel Reame knew, jockeys. Carmine LaRocca was back from the Franciscan monastery he went to every summer to purge himself of ten months of unalloyed drug use. Of course, he took some cocaine with him into the retreat, but purely, he said, as a precaution.

With the exception of poor Tatino Faveri, everyone was back in Milan.

No one would miss the first big event of the new season—Sabina Irone's marriage to a gorgeous young American.

Diana Rau, not one to miss the opportunity of a lifetime, planned to reveal her new line of fashion at sunset, in the Piazza San Babila (thanks to the kind permission of the Office of Urban

Affairs)—having all of fashionable Milan already assembled for the wedding, only an idiot would not take advantage of the timing.

The news of Sabina's wedding had been a big enough bomb to drop onto the world of Bel Reame, but it was as nothing compared to the effect of the announcement of Diana Rau's new fashion house. How could she have kept her secret so effectively!?

Many people expected—or at least hoped—she would fall flat on her face. It was an act of hubris. Maria Teresa di Montenapoleone was especially fearful of being dethroned from her own perch atop the world of fashion. She revelled in being at the top of all the women fashion designers and welcomed a new rival with the same enthusiasm she would feel for a diagnosis of breast cancer. She was sure Diana's sudden emergence on the scene had been engineered by Irone.

Irone was denying the allegation to everyone. Even before people brought up the subject he would disavow any knowledge. "I swear, I was totally in the dark. I had no idea she was planning to do such a thing. The worst part about it is I'm losing a fabulous PR director."

"But you must have known," they would say.

"She never even hinted at it. You think I like the idea of another competitor!"

Of course Irone had known. He'd helped her, in fact, as much as he could without getting directly involved, because he needed Kao's backing in the Far Eastern markets for his own line.

From his Olympian height off in Venice, Zaco Ottoboni looked upon all these developments with amusement. He'd received the two invitations, of course, one to the wedding, the other for the fashion show. There was no question he would attend either, especially on the heels of his recent unpleasant visit to Milan. He was happy Diana was striking out on her own. He enjoyed anything that might ruffle the feathers of the members of Bel Reame. He called Diana to offer his congratulations.

"How does it feel to beard the lions in their own den?"

"I'm sure I'll feel great when this is all over. Right now I'm

236

too busy to feel anything. Are you coming to the show?"

"I'm sorry, my dear, but traveling is not one of the things I do well. You should entertain the idea of doing a show in Venice. Imagine the effect of a fashion show, say, on the Grand Canal."

"That's a great idea. I'll do next year's show there."

"I'll help you all I can. I'm sorry I won't be seeing your debut, but I hope you understand."

"You *will* be able to see this year's show. It's going to be tele-vised live."

"That's an incredible coup! How'd you ever pull that off?"

"All those years in PR have given me an incredible set of contacts—you wouldn't believe the strings that had to be pulled for this broadcast."

"What a triumph! I promise not to miss the show. Good luck, Diana."

As soon as he hung up, Diana fell into a slump. Ottoboni had raised her morale temporarily but she had been pushing herself so hard for so long, she was an absolute bundle of nerves and ten-sions. The slightest thing could set her off these days. She was walk-ing on a wire and she knew it. She knew the speedballs and the coke were gaining on her, and she was afraid she'd collapse before the big day arrived.

She went over to her full-length mirror and was reassured by what greeted her eye. At least the outside is holding up splen-didly, she thought.

She felt much better after scrutinizing her image in the mir-ror. She went to her closet and picked out the dress she would wear for Sabina's wedding and returned to the mirror and held it up in front of herself.

She would have to look smashing that day, anything less would not do. She had designed the dress she was holding up. She looked at herself in the mirror and thought, Positively smashing.

Ciaccio Irone was so deeply moved, he was all but choked up. There was Rick, splendid in his morning suit, standing next to Sabina in a long white gown, trading vows before the bishop of Milan. Ciaccio, off to the right, was on the point of disintegration, tears welling up out of his eyes.

Sabina's home was inundated with bridal gifts. Some of them were beyond anything even she, in her most avaricious dreams, had expected. Ottoboni had sent an exquisite crystal service of antique Venetian blown glass. The Little Lord had sent a solid gold carving tray. The Pipe had sent a medium-size painting by Utrillo—its provenance was very shaky, but they were pleased anyway. Diovisi had sent a Saladin carved in gold and jade.

"I do," said Sabina.

"I do," said Rick.

"I do," whispered Ciaccio under his breath, tears streaming down his cheeks.

"Look how moved the brother is," the Duchess Gandolfi whispered to her niece.

The ceremony was over and everybody was pouring out of the church into the Piazza San Babila, where it was cooler. The weather could not have been more perfect, in fact. It was one of those rare September days when there's not a hint of humidity in the air, and the suggestion of a breeze, pleasant, yet invigorating, wafted its way among the crowd.

Ciaccio hugged his sister. "Sabina, you look radiant. I've never seen you looking more beautiful."

Then he hugged Rick. "I love you," he whispered into Rick's ear as he leaned over to kiss Rick formally on both cheeks.

Rick didn't reply, he merely smiled back. From now on, he was the boss and he might as well start acting that way immediately.

The guests crowded around the bride and groom and best man as they got into the bridal Rolls-Royce to go home and change into the clothes they would travel in. Their plane for Scotland was leaving in three hours.

As soon as the wedding vows were exchanged, Diana Rau cut out from the crowd to go and oversee her fashion show. The television crew was already beginning to set up in the square. Diana was next to frantic with last minute jitters. Luckily she had her coke to calm her down.

Tomorrow, she promised herself, I'll give up all the coke. But, oh, thank God, I have it now when I need it. Of course, if the show's not a success, I won't be needing it tomorrow either. I'll either be dead by a self-inflicted wound or in a sanitarium somewhere.

The sun was setting. Diana's show was reaching its climax. The Piazza San Babila was brightly illuminated by huge floodlights provided by the television station.

Diana was especially pleased with the weather—the evening promised to be as nearly perfect as the afternoon had been. It had gotten a bit cooler, but still well this side of comfortable. Everything was going swimmingly. Led by Inna, who instantly established herself as the star among the models, all the models were doing a magnificent job. They were beautiful, poised and, best of all, classy. Each new creation elicited murmurs of approval and lots of applause from the highly knowledgeable crowd.

Diana was no longer scared. Self-confidence now oozed out of her every pore. She felt strong enough to conquer the world, if need be. Kao kept sending her encouraging smiles. The TV cameras were sending her fashions into millions of homes.

Sandra Marzolini, fashion editor of the evening news, was approaching Diana for an interview. It had all been agreed on in advance. Sandra had submitted a list of all the questions she would ask and Diana had approved of them all.

Nevertheless, all her years of experience in PR abandoned her as she saw Sandra approach. Suddenly she panicked. She'd need some coke to see her through her first nationwide interview on TV. She dashed to her trailer, which was parked nearby. She searched the place frantically but the coke was nowhere to be found. All of a sudden she noticed Kao standing in the doorway.

"Looking for this?" he asked, holding up a big vial of coke—

her vial.

"Give me that!" she said, lunging for the vial.

"Not on your life. Everything is going too smoothly and you've already had more than enough to judge by the unnatural glow in your eyes."

"I need that—I must have some now."

"I'll give it back to you when you don't need it quite so desperately," he said, walking back out into the square.

Cursing Kao, she ran toward the trailer for the models. They all used coke, there would be no trouble finding some there.

Almost instantly, she found some in a makeup kit. She grabbed it and feverishly laid out some lines and sucked them up into her nose. It turned out to be heroin, not coke. So much the better, she thought. This should really calm me down. She returned to her own trailer and took a hefty swig from the gin bottle. Then, just to be on the safe side, she took two uppers.

Now, she was ready to face the cameras.

While the cameraman was adjusting levels and altering the focus, Diana glanced over and looked into the monitor. She looked great. Her skin glowed with freshness, her eyes flashed with a particular brilliance.

The director signaled and they were on.

After introducing Diana, Sandra asked, "Signora Rau, what made you decide to enter the world of designers? Do you think you have something new to add to the world of fashion?"

Diana smiled indulgently. "Not only do I think so, I *know* so. I have a unique vision of how to make women elegant and beautiful and I want to share it with the world."

"Are you pleased with how the show is going?"

"Very. I've been so busy with the models that I haven't had a chance to see the effect it's having on people but from the applause it seems like a success."

Sandra said, "Rest easy, Signora Rau. The show is a smashing success. Everyone's mad about your creations. I'd like to add my own compliment, if I may. I've never seen more beautiful designs.

They're extraordinary."

Trying her best to look modest, Diana said, "Thank you so much. I'm glad you like my work." Meanwhile she was thinking, You poor cow. You couldn't begin to afford my designs. And even if you could it wouldn't improve matters any—I can't work miracles. "You must come to my showroom when it opens next week."

"I will," Sandra said. "One more question, please. Is it true you and Kao Misokubi are engaged to be married?"

It was a hit below the belt. This question wasn't on the pre-approved list.

"He and I are very good friends."

"Is that all you have to say?"

"Thank you, very much," Diana said smiling as she dashed off. Sandra, alone with the camera, proceeded to sing the praises of the show.

The show was almost over. The waves of applause were beginning to sound fatigued. The square was filled with every member of Bel Reame who wasn't flying to Scotland that night and they were acknowledging by their applause that they were welcoming a worthy peer into their ranks. Diana had pulled it off. She was one of them now.

Diana went over to Inna who was trying to get into the closing *pièce de résistance*—a wedding dress. It was gauzy and light and the essence of lace.

"Everything O.K.?" Inna asked, looking up at Diana, half in, half out of the dress.

"Couldn't be better," Diana replied from the stratosphere she was afloat in thanks to the heroin, gin and uppers.

There were only a few minutes until the presentation of the wedding dress. Diana went back to her own trailer.

She lay down on a chaise and closed her eyes. What a blissful day she'd had. It was as close to a total triumph as was humanly possible. What more could she ask for?

The answer rose up out of the mists of her drug-beclouded

241

brain. Andrea. Suddenly she was as miserable as she had been euphoric the moment before.

Goddam, why did she have to think of him now, of all times? Why hadn't he been willing to compromise? He had made no effort to see things from Diana's point of view. After the fashion show, life could be different. She could have restored her relationship with Kao, put it on a business-only basis.

Her misery rose up and engulfed her. Andrea. How she missed him, how much sweeter her triumph would be if he were here to share it.

What was all the success in the world, all the TV coverage in the world, millions of dollars, if she didn't have Andrea? Dust and ashes.

She needed a snort.

She reeled around the trailer looking for her coke for a couple of minutes before it dawned on her that Kao had absconded with it. Goddam Kao!

However, the gin was still there, and the bottle was still half full. She grabbed hold of the bottle and slugged back three good mouthfuls. The gin burned her mouth, even as she felt it coursing through her body. Someone called out. They were shouting her name. The show was coming to an end. It was time for the wedding dress.

Diana glanced at herself in the mirror. The image was oddly blurred, opaque. All she could tell really was that her hair was messed up, from lying down no doubt. What were a few locks of hair out of place? She was still desirably beautiful. She staggered to the door of the trailer.

She found herself needing to hold on to the railing to descend the few steps of the trailer. Outside there was a small clutch of people, mostly models, Kao also. She couldn't make them out very clearly. Why was everything so blurry? They seemed to be staring at her.

Inna, a vision of unalloyed beauty, wearing the wedding gown, appeared at her side. With concern in her voice, she asked, "Diana, are you all right?"

"Couldn't be better. Never felt better in my life."

"Then why are you crying?"

"Don't be silly. I'm not crying. I'm laughing."

She tried to call up a laugh but all that emerged was a grotesque strangulated sob.

Kao reached out for her hand. "Come on, Diana, let's go home. You'll feel better soon." She viciously pushed his hand away. She didn't need anyone, certainly not Kao. Oh, Andrea, she thought, I'd do anything to get you back.

All of a sudden a glimmer appeared in her eyes. She had an inspiration. She'd model the wedding dress herself. Somewhere Andrea must be watching the show on TV. He'd see her in the dress.

"Take it off!" she yelled at Inna.

Inna stared at her, not comprehending.

"Take it off, goddamit!" Diana shouted, starting to pull the dress off Inna.

Inna obeyed, reluctantly. She had no choice—otherwise, Diana would rip the dress apart. Inna got out of the dress and Diana snatched it and clumsily started putting it on herself. Her left shoe caught in the train and the heel was pulled off. It didn't matter.

"Move. Get out of my way," she yelled to the people in front of her. They were all staring at her now, horrified. Inna burst into tears.

"Stop it, Diana. Get control of yourself," Kao said as commandingly as he could.

"Let me go!" Diana pulled away from him violently. She dashed to the square, running behind the stage.

Everything was in place for the grand finale—the spotlights, the TV cameras, the still photographers, the applauding crowd.

Diana lurched forward. No one dared to stop her. They all stood there frozen, unable to help—all the secretaries, the dressers, the backstage crew.

Sandra Marzolini realized something was wrong, something was alarmingly wrong.

"Cut!" she shouted to the cameraman.

"Keep rolling!" shouted Manuel de Varga, the Spanish director who had a genius for the dramatic moment, the telling detail.

Diana stepped out on stage.

What she thought she looked like was anyone's guess. What appeared before the eyes of one and all was a mess of an outfit, worn by a woman who looked and walked like a zombie, with the dark, cavernous, haunted eyes of a ghoul. The ripped wedding dress looked positively wretched, and the broken heel made her limp grotesquely.

Diana advanced along the runway toward the crowd. A ripple of laughter appeared in the crowd, and like a stone thrown into a pond, it spread through the audience, growing in force as it spread. Hearing laughter, Diana joined in, waving her arms in what she thought was a triumphant gesture over her head. The cameras kept their eyes on her progress, and that image, ludicrous in the extreme, was beamed to millions of households across the country.

The new rising star in the fashion firmament had been transformed into a black hole in the fashion universe, all in the course of a couple of hours.

Inna was sobbing uncontrollably. Someone handed her a glassine bag filled with a white powder.

Ah, thought Inna, just what I need.